To all the gorgeously sophisticated French actresses (and one in particular) who have entertained me throughout the years and have inspired the character of Camille.

CHAPTER ONE

"You're here bright and early this morning," Josephine says before I can even place my order.

"Walk of shame?" Micky butts in.

"Christ, ladies. I'll have a coffee first, we can talk after."

Micky looks at her watch. "I've never seen you here this early."

Josephine elbows her in the biceps. "A large black coffee for Zoya, please."

"Coming right up." Micky gets busy with the coffee machine.

"How are you today, Jo?" I ask.

"Very well, thank you."

"I suppose it's out of the question for me to call Caitlin at this ungodly hour and ask her to join me?"

"You can try, but she wasn't awake when I left." She quirks up her eyebrows.

I wave my credit card over the terminal to pay for my coffee. "I won't bother then." I check my phone in case I missed a text message while ordering. The screen is blank. "Myrtle is sick and there appears to be a bit of a problem in my Airbnb down the street. The new occupant arrived late last night and is complaining the smoke detector is beeping every few seconds. I promised to change the batteries first thing."

"Here you go." Micky hands me my coffee.

"If I lived in Darlinghurst, I could have stopped by last

night."

"Such a pity you don't know anyone in the area." Micky smirks.

"Very funny. They arrived after midnight. I wasn't going to rouse any of you because my caretaker was sick, was I?"

"Thank goodness for that," Micky replies.

Rebecca used to deal with all of this, I want to say but swallow the words, because I don't want to talk about my ex. It's too early in the morning for that particular kind of grievance.

"I'll become your neighbor soon enough." I sip from the coffee. "Just need to sort out some stuff first."

A sudden break-up from your partner of sixteen years is emotionally harrowing enough even without all the practical things to arrange: assets to divide, and figure out who gets which souvenir from that trip to Tasmania. As far as I'm concerned, Rebecca can have it all, as long as I never have to see her face again. My lawyer disagrees.

"One of the houses in my street is for sale," Micky says.

I perk up my ears. "Really?"

"Yeah, I'll get you the number of the agent. You should check it out."

"Maybe I will." My phone buzzes. "Ah, here we go." I check the message. "Time to go." I drain my coffee, give Micky and Josephine a wave, and make my way to the apartment I own but haven't set foot in for months.

———

The apartment is above a hair salon, which is still closed. I suppose no one wants to get their hair cut before eight o'clock in the morning. I take the stairs to the first floor and knock gently on the door, shuffling my weight from foot to foot. I never wanted to own a bloody Airbnb. Another thing I resent Rebecca for. Just add it to the pile.

The door flies open and a woman stands in front of me. She's tall and has cheekbones for days, but what I notice most of all are her eyes. Not the color, but how they sparkle with something. I hope it's not rage. I think it best to immediately launch into an apology.

"I'm so sorry about this." I give her my widest TV smile and hold out my hand. "Hi, I'm Zoya. Your smoke detector battery replacer for today."

The woman looks at my hand for a split second, then takes it in hers and gives it a quick, firm shake, her fingers squeezing tightly. "Camille." She steps aside to let me in.

I look around. A high-pitched beep startles me.

"It's been like that all night," Camille says with a heavy French accent. Her hands are on her hips. "Not exactly conducive to a good night's sleep."

"I can imagine. Let me take care of this." I look up at the smoke detector. A red light blinks. I don't remember the ceiling being so high. Is there a ladder somewhere in this building? This whole scene is making me feel extremely inadequate. Rebecca was always the handy, super-organized one—a skill that allowed her to organize her affair around our life together for more than a year. I was just the fool who didn't have a clue.

Just when I think I'm putting the whole sordid ordeal behind me, something like this happens to remind me of it. This apartment was Rebecca's project from the start. Why it is up to me to deal with it now remains a mystery.

I scan the kitchen for a chair. I step out of my shoes and balance on it precariously. Camille scrutinizes my every move. I raise my hands but I can't reach the ceiling.

I climb off the chair. "Looks like we're going to need something higher."

She gives me a look I can't decipher. "I'll try. I'm taller than you."

"Thanks." Why don't we keep spare batteries in this apartment? I'll have to talk to Myrtle. Or just sell the damn place. Then I wouldn't be standing here in bare feet in front of a woman who is probably pretty pissed off at me. Although she hides it quite well.

I watch her clamber upon the chair. She does it gracefully, as if balancing on a piece of furniture is all she does in life. She stands on tiptoe and can just reach the outer shell of the smoke detector with her fingertips.

"Careful." I steady the chair for her.

She has already screwed off the outer casing. "Hand me the batteries."

I try to pull the package open but, as always with these things, it's hard to find a spot to pierce it and I have to tear at it with all my might. I finally manage to pry out two batteries. Our fingers touch when I hold them up to her.

She drops the old batteries in my palm and, all the while balancing on the tips of her toes, replaces the batteries and screws the lid on again.

I hold out my hand to her for support when she climbs back down and she takes it. At least I've done something.

"That wasn't so hard, was it?" she says.

I shake my head. "I'm mortified. Really. I will reimburse you for the night. The person who usually takes care of this is indisposed at the moment and, as you've clearly noticed, I'm not very good at any of this."

She waves me off. "Just an idea. Keep some spare batteries in a kitchen drawer, perhaps? I could have done this myself last night if I'd had the necessary equipment."

"I can't apologize enough. You must be so tired. How about I take you out for coffee? Show you what's where in the neighborhood?" My earlobes flush. I don't even know the area that well. The best I can do is take her to the Pink Bean and hope Kristin is there to tell her all about Darlinghurst's best spots.

Camille ponders my question. "Okay," she says. "Give me five minutes." She heads into the bathroom.

I put the chair back and leave the remaining batteries on the kitchen counter.

Maybe when I see the real estate agent to view the house Micky was talking about, I can ask her to come and take a look at this place. Or maybe I should just move in here. I glance around. No, I couldn't. Rebecca's touch is all over the decor. That turquoise contrast wall in the living area. The photograph of an outback road in Queensland to my right. It used to hang in our house, until she redecorated it and relocated it here.

"I'm ready for that coffee." Camille exits the bathroom with a smile.

CHAPTER TWO

The Pink Bean is too busy for Micky and Josephine to ask me prying questions so they have to content themselves with inquisitive stares, which I ignore. I buy coffee and a couple of croissants and Camille and I sit.

"How long are you staying in Sydney?" I ask.

She chuckles. "I'm staying in your rental apartment. You should know."

I shake my head. "It's a long story why I don't have a clue about any of this."

"So, I can stay as long as I like." Camille tips her cup back. "You wouldn't even notice."

"I probably wouldn't." I push the plate with croissants in her direction.

"Thanks. I'm famished." She picks one up and tears off a corner. Before she puts it in her mouth, she says, "Croissants in Sydney are surprisingly not disappointing."

"You're the expert, I guess." I look at her as she chews. She seems so at ease. So unperturbed by what happened. "Are you here for work or pleasure?"

"Definitely pleasure." She nods slowly. "I flew in from Brisbane last night. I've spent the past two months in your beautiful country. Sydney is my last stop before I go back to France."

"Ah, that's why you're so Zen."

She slants her head. "Perhaps. Only a week left to relax." Her cheeks dimple when she grins.

"Where in France are you from?"

"*Paris.*" She pronounces it the French way. "Born and bred. But as much as I love it, sometimes you just need to get away."

"If you can, then, yes, I guess." I wish I could have run away from Sydney after Rebecca told me she was leaving me.

"I believe that if you really want to, you can." She rips off another piece of croissant. "Are you sick of Sydney?" Her eyes bore into me.

"Not Sydney so much as certain people who live here."

She purses her lips together and nods. "I think I know exactly what you mean. But let me guess. Your children and your job prevent you from going away for a longer time. And your Airbnb property, of course." She follows up with a chuckle.

I laugh at her dig. "No children, but my job is pretty demanding."

"Whose isn't these days?" She sighs.

It's refreshing to talk to an interesting woman, who, at first glance, looks like she could be the perfect demographic for my TV show but doesn't have a clue of who I am. "What do you do?"

"I work for the CNRS, the *Centre National de la Recherche Scientifique.* I advise the French government on scientific matters."

"That sounds important."

"It's a big responsibility. Of course, my advice gets ignored half the time, but I take my position very seriously." She curls her lips into a smile. "But one of my mantras for this trip was to talk about work as little as possible. Even though it's inevitable when you travel alone, meet people and make casual conversation. It's usually the first thing that comes up."

"That's the world we live in. We're defined not by who we are but what we do."

"Very true." She holds up her hands. "So please excuse

me for asking, but what is it that you do?"

"I'm a television presenter. I interview people."

"Like a chat show?" Not even a cool Frenchwoman can resist perking up at finding out she's sitting across from someone who gets her face on television.

"A bit more in-depth than that. My show is not a promotion vehicle for actors and the like. We have one guest per week and the actual interview takes hours to produce. The research takes weeks."

"You must know a whole lot about many people then." She leans back in her chair.

"Too much at times." I smile at Camille. I like her. There's something very disarming about her.

"Do you get recognized all the time?"

"Not that much, actually. This is not America. People are still pretty discreet. And my show doesn't have a big viewership among the selfie generation."

Camille jots out her lip and nods. "Looks like I have some googling to do."

"There should be complimentary wi-fi in the apartment," I say. "I hope it's working."

"It is." She cracks a smile. "Don't feel too bad about the smoke detector. Your place is really nice. This is coming from someone who has sampled a vast array of accommodation all over the country the past couple of months. I wanted a really nice place to stay for my last stop and I'm not disappointed."

"Thanks for saying that." I make eye-contact for a brief moment.

"So please explain to me how a TV personality is sitting here having coffee with me this morning after trying to change the batteries in the smoke detector. Somehow, it doesn't compute."

"I'm a very down-to-earth kind of girl who likes to get her hands dirty." Camille seems like the sort of person who can appreciate a joke.

"Right." She nods, her face serious. "I could tell as soon

as you climbed onto that chair. Such confidence."

We both chuckle. "The person who usually deals with all of this for me has pneumonia. Poor thing."

"Good morning, Zoya and friend." Kristin appears next to our table. "Can I get you anything else?"

I jump at the opportunity to introduce Camille to Kristin, who knows everything there is to know about Darlinghurst—where to drink, where to eat, and where to have coffee, of course.

While they chat, I consider asking Kristin if *she* wants to buy the flat. She is the kind of person who would have everything in perfect working order all the time. And she and Sheryl only live three feet away. Then my mind wanders to this afternoon's mediation meeting with Rebecca and our respective lawyers. If only I could send someone else to sort that all out for me as well.

Kristin asks Camille to stop by after the morning rush so she can give her some more information, and says goodbye. We both follow her with our eyes as she heads to the counter. Just then Sheryl appears for her morning coffee before she heads to work. She kisses Kristin fully on the mouth.

"Oh," Camille says.

"If you hadn't noticed yet, Darlinghurst is extremely gay friendly."

"I only arrived late last night." Camille has suddenly lost some of her easy conversation skills. "I didn't really get a chance to notice."

I hope I'm not sitting across from a homophobe. She may look like the nicest woman on the planet, it wouldn't mean a thing. I've heard the vilest things come from the mouths of the most educated, cultured-looking people. Hatred comes in all sorts of disguises.

"You seem to know the owner well. Do you live around here?" Camille has apparently regrouped.

"Not yet, but I plan to. Sheryl, Kristin's partner"—I nod

in the direction of the counter where Sheryl is waiting for her takeaway cup—"and I have a good friend in common, who moved to Darlinghurst six months ago and I've been jealous ever since. It's time for a change of scenery for me, anyway."

I think of my—our—house in Balmain. How empty and big it feels when I come home these days.

"I can recommend taking a few months off. It does wonders for your perspective," Camille says. "It helps that Australians are possibly the friendliest people I've come across."

"We do our best." I give her a wide smile.

"Have you lived in Sydney all your life?"

"I grew up in Perth, where most of my family still live. My great-grandparents immigrated here from India."

"I went to Perth," Camille says. "At the beginning of my trip, which feels like two years instead of two months ago."

My phone starts ringing in my bag. "Sorry, it's probably work."

I check the screen and the name of my lawyer comes up.

"Zoya, can we do two instead of three this afternoon?" She's a matter-of-fact woman who has no time for pleasantries. "I'm asking on behalf of Miss Firth's lawyer."

I exhale a deep sigh. "Sure. Let's get it over with as quickly as possible."

"Okay. See you then." She hangs up.

"Typical," I murmur under my breath.

"Everything okay?" Camille inquires.

"All part of that long story I hinted at earlier. My ex driving me up the wall." I try to block out the negative thoughts by folding my lips into a big smile. It doesn't really work, but the story of my separation from Rebecca is not something to impose on my Airbnb guest. "I should probably leave you to it now." I took the day off so I could mentally prepare for this meeting. I haven't seen Rebecca in months. "You have my number. Please call me if you need anything at all."

I rise and so does Camille.

"Thank you for the coffee and croissants. I appreciate the gesture."

While we shake hands, I say, "Maybe I'll see you around before you leave. If not, I hope you have a wonderful stay."

Our hands linger. I glance at her face—so pleasant and relaxed—one more time, then head out the door.

CHAPTER THREE

"Can we talk in private?" Rebecca asks after the meeting has drawn to a close. I tuned out for most of it. Even though Rebecca and I are not legally married, we own a house together and everything we have is tangled up with each other. But she's the one who cheated, left me, and moved out. For my lawyer, it seems to make all the difference as to who gets what.

But I'm not interested in hanging onto any material possessions we shared. Neither is she, apparently. She was quick to agree to sell the house. Now that we've both signed the agreement, we can finally put it on the market. I can move on for real.

When we bought the rental apartment, the accountant advised us to put it in my name, so I'm stuck with that. Rebecca didn't even flinch when it came up in the meeting, even though she's the one who did all the work. She's probably feeling guilty.

"Yeah, sure," I say.

"Do you want to go for a coffee?"

"Do you have time for that? You asked to move the meeting an hour earlier."

"Because I wanted to have time for a chat with you. We haven't talked in so long."

I scoff. "And whose fault is that?" I hope she doesn't spin me a line asking to remain friends or something outrageous like that.

"Maybe something stronger than coffee?"

"Fine."

We say goodbye to our lawyers, who are getting a big fat check for not doing much at all, seeing as at least this part of our separation is very amicable. It's the other, non-material parts that have been the most violent.

I follow Rebecca to a bar down the street, suspecting her of having scouted it beforehand, because she doesn't even have to look around to find a place for us to have that drink.

"How's Julie?" I ask, my voice dripping with sarcasm.

"What can I get you? Chardonnay?" She ignores my question.

I nod and watch her walk off. It still hurts. It's been almost six months now, but there walks a woman I believed I knew through and through. A woman who told me she loved me nearly every day of our life together. A woman who lied. A woman who broke my heart into a million pieces. The worst part of it all is, after she'd been sleeping with Julie for close to a year, and finally had found the courage to tell me—and leave me in the process—she made it sound as though it was all my fault.

She returns with two wine glasses filled to the brim.

"To it officially all being over." I raise my glass.

Rebecca doesn't raise her glass. She just drinks. "Thanks for being so agreeable about all the legal stuff."

"It's not because I'm a scorned woman that I have to behave like one."

Rebecca cocks her head. "Do you think we can have a conversation without the sarcasm?"

"Oh, are you going to be the mature one this time?"

"Please, I'm begging you, Zoya. I just want to talk. We just divided our assets. Can we just be civilized for ten minutes?"

"Fine." I look away. The bar is empty this time of the day.

"I just wanted to check in with you. See how you're doing," Rebecca says.

When I look into her eyes, it's as though I can see all the good times we had together. We were so happy for such a long time. Was I really the one who fucked it all up? Who drove her into the arms of another woman?

"Maybe I should take a sabbatical. Get out of the country for a bit. Maybe travel through India. Connect with my roots."

"I still worry about you, even though we're not together anymore," Rebecca says.

"How nice of you." The words just come out. I have no idea how to curb my bitter tongue. "Do you worry about me when you and Julie change the channel when my show comes on? Do you worry about me when you fall asleep with your arm around her? Every time she fills the space I used to take up in your life?"

"You're clearly not ready for this."

"I don't think I'll ever be."

"I've apologized so many times already. I can't see how me saying I'm sorry again will help, so I'm kind of at the end of my wits here." Rebecca drinks from her wine in long gulps.

"What do you want from me? Why are we even sitting here? Can't you see it's just one big reminder of how things used to be, before... *you-know-who.*"

"Julie is my partner now, Zoya." She sighs. "And you keep referring to how things used to be, but I think you're forgetting that, in the end, they were not that great."

"Oh, here we go again."

"No, here *you* go again."

"This was clearly a mistake." I push the glass of wine away.

"Clearly." Rebecca looks like she's had enough as well. It's strange to think that there used to be a time, not even so long ago, that we couldn't get enough of each other's company. That we believed we'd be together forever. How quickly things can change.

"I don't want things to be like this between us." She injects some softness into her voice. "You are still important to me."

"Maybe you should have thought of that before you started banging someone else." I get up. "And it's easy for you to say what you want and how I'm still important to you and yadda, yadda, yadda, when you get to go home to your new girlfriend after this, and all I have is an empty house, in which everything reminds me of us. You left me with nothing. And you took my self-esteem along with you as well." I curse myself for the last sentence.

"I know it's hard." Her voice breaks.

"I hadn't exactly expected to find myself single again on the cusp of fifty."

"I know. But you're Zoya Das. You must have women lining up for you."

"Please, don't give me that superficial bullshit. You're only saying it to make yourself feel better, anyway. To ease your guilt because the fact remains that you cheated on me for an entire year. Well, guess what? You will always be guilty of that and no matter how many times you say you're sorry, I will never forgive you for it."

I hear some shuffling behind the bar. The bartender is looking in our direction.

"I'd better go. I'll let you know when an offer comes in for the house."

Rebecca is silent. It reminds me of the silence she shrouded herself in as she was packing her things after she first told me. That fateful day my whole life came crumbling down.

"I wanted to strangle and kiss her at the same time," I say.

"Maybe you should take one of Amber's yoga classes. Even Josephine is a fan now," Caitlin says, as she presents me with a tumbler of whiskey.

"Oh sure, me lined up next to a bunch of happy lesbian couples. I mean, even you are monogamous now, for crying out loud. What has the world come to?"

Caitlin rolls her eyes. "Aw, poor Zoya Das. Poor little rich girl." She shoots me a look over the rim of her glass. "I understand you're upset. Today was an emotional day. And Rebecca truly fucked you over. But you need to move on."

"Move on? And pretend I didn't just split from the love of my life? Pretend it doesn't still hurt me every minute of every day?"

"Yes. You'll have to pretend at first. But, you know, have a fling, at least. Do something that makes you feel good about yourself. That makes you feel desired. It works wonders for the self-esteem."

"I'm not like you, Caitlin. No offense."

"Definitely none taken, my dear friend."

"I used to be so many things to her and now someone else is and that hurts. It makes me feel so replaceable. So insignificant. And sometimes, I even think she was right to blame it all on me."

"At the moment, I'm not a big Rebecca fan because she treated you so disrespectfully, but I really don't think she blamed it all on you."

"You know what I mean."

Caitlin shakes her head. "You know my view on this."

"Yeah, well, where were you when I needed your help with all of this? Shagging your way across the United States, no doubt." I glance at Caitlin from under my lashes. My bitterness might be getting the best of me.

"How long has it been?"

"What?"

"When was the last time you got laid, sister?" Caitlin puts on a funny accent.

I scoff. Good question, actually. I follow up with a shrug.

"I guarantee you, you will feel so much better about yourself—and you'll stop attacking me, your good friend—after you've had another woman's hands all over you."

"Oh my god." It's my time to roll my eyes. "Like sex is the solution to everything. I'm so sick of hearing that."

"Suit yourself." Caitlin puts her glass down. "Maybe you're not ready. Although I'm a big believer in not waiting until you think you might be."

"I wouldn't even know where to start. I can't just go to a bar and pick someone up."

"Why not?" Caitlin challenges me. From the look on her face, I can tell she's getting some glee out of this. Or she already knows what I'm going to answer.

"You know why."

"Don't tell me because you're Zoya Das. If anything, it will help."

I shake my head. "You know I'm not really one for one-night stands."

"It's never too late to change your mind about these things."

"Caitlin, I respect your choices, but I have my own views on sex and monogamy. We've had this conversation so many times before."

"Basically, what you're saying is that you want to wait until you fall in love again. From where I'm sitting, it looks like that might take a good long while. You're a long way from being over Rebecca."

"No matter what she says... for me, it just came so out of the blue, you know?"

"Yeah."

"But that's enough about me." I need to refocus my attention. "Let's talk about you. How are things with you and Jo?"

"Good, though she works too much. She's got two singing gigs this weekend and—"

My phone beeps, indicating I received a text message. I

try to ignore it.

Caitlin looks at my phone then back at me again. "Jo and I are doing fine. I really have nothing to complain about."

My phone beeps again because I haven't read the message yet.

"Sorry. Let me just have a look." I feel a bit pissed at myself because I'm usually the first one to scold anyone too glued to their phone to conduct a proper conversation.

I googled you, the message says. *And now I would really like to see you again. Camille.*

A smile stretches across my face.

"What is it?" Caitlin asks.

"The woman who's staying in the rental. I met her this morning. She says she would *really* like to see me again."

Caitlin holds up her hands. "There you go. Just as we're talking about it, the perfect opportunity presents itself. It must be serendipity."

"I... don't know." I make a mental note to google myself later, just to see what Camille has dug up on me. Probably all the salacious details of my split from Rebecca.

"Tell me about her," Caitlin asks.

"She's French, has been traveling through Australia for the past two months. She has some government science job. That's about all I know."

"Is she cute?"

"Cute? She's a French woman of a certain age. I hardly think the word *cute* applies."

"Okay, so you think she's pretty. Good." Caitlin smirks. "Go for it. Take her to dinner tonight. Do something to make yourself feel better."

"Tonight? It's six o'clock and I'm in no state to have dinner with a stranger right now."

"You can get ready here. I'll lend you something fabulous from my wardrobe, but I wouldn't worry about that too much if she's been living out of a suitcase for so many weeks. Just… distract yourself. Perhaps dinner with an enigmatic French tourist is exactly what you need right now. To forget about Rebecca. Give her the finger, so to speak."

"If you don't stop soon, you may well convince me to go."

"You want to. I can tell. She's asking you out. Just go for it."

I see Camille's reaction to Kristin and Sheryl's kiss this morning in a different light now. Perhaps she was suddenly wondering about *my* sexuality. Googling me must have given her all the answers. "What should I text back?" My phone feels heavy in my hand.

"A resounding *Yes*." Caitlin sits there smiling.

"Where should I take her? It's Friday night. Can I still get a good booking somewhere?"

"Tell you what," Caitlin says. "You text her back. Tell her to meet you outside the Pink Bean at seven. While you spruce yourself up, I'll take care of everything."

I hold up my glass. "Why thank you, my friend. I'm also going to need another drink."

Caitlin shoots me a big grin. Whatever her plan was, it worked.

CHAPTER FOUR

Caitlin has booked us into a new gastropub halfway between her building and the Pink Bean. Even though it's still quite early for a Friday, the place is already heaving when we arrive. I wonder if she had to pull any strings—or drop any names —to secure us a table. But I'm not too concerned with any of that, because I'm seeing Camille in a whole new light tonight. She's no longer the woman who's renting my apartment. She's my date.

"Welcome Miss Das and lovely friend," a bearded hipster-waiter says. "My name is Thomas and I'll be serving you tonight."

We follow him to a table in the covered courtyard in the back, which is surrounded by trees lit up with fairy lights. A candle is already burning on our table. Did Caitlin request a romantic atmosphere when she made the reservation?

Out of sheer embarrassment, I'm inclined to say a friend set this all up, but then I remember Caitlin's words when she ushered me out the door. "You've got absolutely nothing to lose," she said. She was right. I've already lost the love of my life. And I need to take my mind off her.

"Very nice." Camille sits down while a wide smile spreads on her lips. "I'm impressed. It feels like I'm somewhere in the French countryside."

"I still owe you for a bad night's sleep, so…" Our gazes cross for a split second.

"You don't owe me a thing, Zoya." She says my name in

a voice so soft, I can barely hear her. But I do. It's like walking into this courtyard has transported me to somewhere else entirely—maybe the French countryside. A place where my heart no longer feels so broken.

The waiter brings us the menu. Though he's trying to be discreet, I can tell he has connected my name to my face. It's always in the little things, like an unexpected nod or a gaze that lingers. As long as he doesn't wink.

"They have some excellent wines," Camille says. "Do you prefer red or white?"

"Whichever one you pick is fine with me." I'm not going to argue with a Frenchwoman about wine, even though most of the wines on the list are from Australia and New Zealand.

"I actually tried this pinot gris just a couple of weeks ago. If it wasn't such a silly undertaking to send a case of wine from here to France, I would have bought some." She finds my gaze. "Is that wine okay with you?"

"Of course."

She calls for Thomas and orders the bottle. When he comes back we order a couple of delicious-sounding dishes. Then I can't hold my curiosity any longer.

"So, you googled me, huh?"

She sinks her teeth into her bottom lip and gives a slow nod. "Very interesting."

"So now you know all about me and I don't know anything about you."

"You mean to say you didn't google me? You, the journalist?" she says with a chuckle in her voice. "You keep surprising me."

"You mean my ignorance about certain things?" I try to look apologetic. "I had a crazy day and…" I pause. "I don't even know your last name."

"It's in the Airbnb reservation." She holds up her glass of wine. "To my advantage in knowledge."

I clink the rim of my glass against hers. "You really do

22

have to tell me what you found out. I won't be able to relax if you don't."

She takes a sip. "Hm, that's really good." Then puts her glass down and leans over the table a little. "You are Zoya Das, of the TV show with the same name. You've won numerous awards. You are actually a journalist and not, as you said, a TV presenter. You are an out and proud lesbian, who recently separated from her long-time partner. And you have no clue how to change the batteries in household appliances." She slants back. "That's about it."

"All true." I lean over the table a little as well. "You must have avoided certain websites."

"I have a pretty good sense of what is true and what isn't."

"That's an excellent quality to have." I drink from the wine Camille has picked. It's light and smooth and goes down well.

"Some things you have no choice but to learn. Not paying attention to gossip magazines is one of them."

"Are prominent scientists often the subject of slander in France?" I ask.

"Only the ones going through a well-documented divorce from a high-profile politician."

"Ah." I could kick myself for not doing any research on her. "Is that why you needed to get away from it all?"

She nods. "This is my *Eat, Pray, Love* journey." She smirks. "Except I drank more than I ate. I don't actually pray and there have been no occurrences of romantic love, though I have fallen in love with your country a little."

Because of my job, I'm pretty well versed in the names of high-profile politicians from other countries, but I still don't know Camille's last name. I'm very much wondering if said politician is a man or a woman. Surely, if it were a woman, it would have caught my attention.

"There's really no need for us French to be so snobbish about our wine, for example." She picks up her glass again.

"This one's better than the product of many a home-grown grape." Camille's eyes narrow as she smiles.

I can't make head nor tail of this woman. It's time to go into interview mode. Start with gentle, innocent questions. Then slowly amp up the depth and breadth and find out what it is I really want to know.

"As far as praying goes, my friend Amber is the best yoga teacher I've ever had, if you want a crash course in that particular practice."

"I'm leaving in a few days. I think it better to focus on the other two pillars of my journey." The gleam of the fairy lights above us catches in her eyes, makes them sparkle with something.

"Aren't you supposed to go to different parts of the world for each? I strongly believe Australian food is underrated, but not many people come here expecting culinary orgasms."

Camille chuckles. "I've had great meals here. And encountered wonderful hospitality. I dread arriving at Charles de Gaulle airport and facing all that French grumpiness again." She shakes her head. "But I really must stop talking in clichés, lest you get the wrong idea of my country. We have our obvious problems, but I love France." A melancholy look crosses her face. "And I miss my children. My daughter is giving birth to her first child in two months. I'm going to be a grandmother."

"Surely you're not old enough for that." I know how cheesy that sounds and take a quick sip from my wine, hoping my comment will dissolve into nothing as I drink.

Camille tilts her head as if to say, yet here I am.

Thomas arrives with our dishes. Crispy bone-marrow for Camille and a fancy chorizo stew for me.

"Ah, that's what I'm talking about," Camille says. She forks some of the bone marrow onto a slice of toast and tucks in. "*Délicieux*," she says with her mouth half full. Once she has swallowed the bite, she says, "You must try this. It would be a crime not to."

I watch as she prepares me a bite, takes the piece of toast in her hand, and holds it in front of my mouth. As I part my lips, the sensuality of her action sends a shiver up my spine. Maybe Caitlin was right. Maybe it has been too long. Why else would a woman feeding me a slice of bread unsettle me so much?

I nod while I chew. She looks at me expectantly.

"How did you say that? *Déliciose?*" I massacre the French pronunciation.

"Close enough." Camille grins.

———

"My husband cheated on me for almost as long as we were married," Camille says. "So I have a pretty good idea of what you're going through right now."

We've finished our meals and polished off the first bottle of wine. Camille insisted I pick the second one and I've gone for a shiraz she seems to approve of. Conversation has been light and, so far, I've only managed to extract that she is, indeed, recently divorced from a man. Her current statement comes out of the blue, just after Thomas has cleared away our plates.

"How long were you married?" I ask.

"Twenty-six very long years."

"Blimey." I'm tipsy enough to have the audacity to ask the more probing questions now. "Were you ever happy in your marriage?"

"The first few years, I was. I didn't yet know about his philandering. We had our children." Her voice sounds a little deeper, devoid of its previous lightness. "That was a good time."

"Why did you stay with him for so long?"

"Because I was young and stupid and naive. Mainly stupid, though." She sips from her wine again, clearly eager to continue the *Drink* part of her journey. "Like all things in life, it was complicated. Well, at least I believed it was. Jean-

Claude was a very promising politician. Older than me and already very much on the rise when we met and then married." She waves her hand. "It's a really long story I don't feel like talking about on this lovely evening... in lovely company." She straightens her posture.

"Why did you ask me out?" I study her face while I wait for her reply. The skin in the corner of her eyes crinkles.

"Because I was very charmed by you and I wouldn't have forgiven myself if I hadn't at least asked. I hadn't really expected you to say yes, after what I found out about your recent break-up."

"It has been six months. That's half a year." I can't believe I'm saying this. "When I got your text, I believed it was because you had your suspicions confirmed that I'm a lesbian."

"That too." She sucks her bottom lip into her mouth for a second. "From doing a bit of research on you, I believed we had quite a few things in common."

I try to phrase my next question as tactfully as possible. "But you were married to a man for twenty-six years."

"Correct." She pauses. "Emphasis on *were*."

"Are you trying to say that this long trip to a country on the other side of the world was about more than getting away? Are you, er, finding yourself?" I sound ridiculous. My interview skills don't thrive on wine and sitting across from a gorgeous woman who has just started flirting with me.

"I *found* myself a long time ago. I just didn't have the courage to do anything about it." She scoffs. "But then something amazing happened in France. We elected a president who is not only an out lesbian, but was in a very similar position to mine not long before she ran for office."

"Dominique Laroche." I can't keep the admiration out of my tone. "One hell of a woman."

"I said to myself, if the president can do it, and face all that public scrutiny, be ridiculed by the old boys' club, and stand proud with her partner next to her while taking the oath, then what's stopping me?"

"She's such an inspiration." I can feel myself light up when I talk about Laroche. "I keep dreaming she'll come on a state visit to Australia and I'll get to interview her on my show."

"Never say never." Camille's eyes are really sparkling now. "Jean-Claude is a minister in her cabinet. We've met many times over the years and we're well acquainted."

"You know Dominique Laroche?" My eyes widen.

"I was at her victory party, crying my eyes out. Not only because I wanted her to win so badly, but even more so because I took it as a sign."

"Wow." It's all I can say, that's how stunned I am.

"I hope that answers your question." She quirks up her eyebrows.

"In a way I couldn't possibly have imagined." Maybe it's the wine, or the fairy lights, but most likely it's simply sitting across from Camille, listening to her accented tones and getting to know her better, but I feel enchanted. Enraptured. And to think I didn't want to come tonight. I was going to catch up on work. Watch television. Or just stay at Caitlin's and get wasted while I remained pissed off at Rebecca.

"I knew it was a long shot, but…" Camille pauses. "I'm very attracted to you."

"You're wooing me."

"I feel like I have no choice." Her voice goes low. "I'm on the clock and I have no time to waste."

"Every minute is precious." I gaze into her eyes and I know she feels the same way. I actively remind myself of Caitlin's words. I truly have nothing to lose. I only stand to gain. Despite claiming, only a few hours ago, that I'm not a one-night stand kind of person. But this is different. This is a woman passing through. A unique opportunity. What did Caitlin call it? Serendipity. Camille is sexy and smart and I find even the tiniest movements she makes with her hands sensual. I want her. I still don't know her last name, but it doesn't matter. It's time to put Caitlin's theory to the test. Will I feel like a different person once I've had another woman's hands all over me?

"I have an idea," Camille whispers. "Why don't we take the rest of this bottle up to the flat? I'm under the impression you need to reacquaint yourself with the place."

"Let me get the check." My heart beats in my throat. I haven't felt this alive in years.

CHAPTER FIVE

"Listen," Camille says when we enter the apartment. "No annoying beeping sound. It's heavenly."

"Thanks to the masterful and swift service of the owner."

"No doubt." She takes two wine glasses out of the kitchen cabinet.

I take the bottle out of the bag Thomas put it in and pour us both a glass. What is the protocol for this? It's been more than sixteen years since my first time with a new woman. I'm guessing that instead of familiarity and the kind of intense intimacy it creates, this encounter will be fueled by desire driven by the new and unfamiliar. It's exciting, but also rather scary.

We make our way into the lounge, where I'm instantly reminded of Rebecca's taste in interior design. It's classy and functional and pretty, like she is. But it comes across as a little soulless now. Generic and devoid of coziness. Was it really this afternoon that I sat across from her in that bar in the CBD? It feels like forever ago. Just like it feels like years ago that she left me and broke my heart.

"It's a nice enough place," I say, just to break the silence.

"It's very comfortable." Camille sets her wine glass down on the coffee table. She holds her hand out for mine. I give it to her.

As she takes the glass from me with one hand, her other one wraps itself around mine. "Just so we're on the same page, I'm going to kiss you now."

"I would like that very much." I tilt my head and lean in. It's been too long since I've felt another woman's lips against mine. Too long since I've felt someone's desire when their mouth opened for me. When our lips meet, I feel it all the way to the pit of my stomach. And it doesn't stop there. I'm immediately compelled to wrap my arms around her neck, draw her closer to me. Even though this can only be a very short-lived fling, the effect a single kiss is having on me is already unmistakable.

Camille's tongue dances in my mouth. She tastes of wine, mostly, but also of something I can't put my finger on. She tastes decidedly unlike Rebecca, who I'm ready to exorcize from my soul—via Camille. I don't just want this— feverishly, madly. I need it. One kiss and already I've got past the point of no return.

When we break from our lip-lock, I find her gaze.

"Just so you know, I haven't been with anyone else since Rebecca and I split," I say, needing this moment of honesty.

Camille hesitates. "I haven't gone all the way with a woman ever before."

"Are you serious?" I have to keep my jaw from dropping.

"I had a fling once, but it remained platonic. For some foolish reason, I've always taken my marriage vows very seriously."

"Loyalty is a quality to be admired."

"Not when it's blind with ignorance." She puts some distance between us, retreats a little.

"Hey, it doesn't matter. The past doesn't matter right now. Only this moment is important."

She breaks out into a soft smile. "Is this the *Pray* moment of my journey?"

"Yes," I say, "let's pray." I shuffle closer to her, able to completely ignore that I'm sitting on a couch Rebecca picked out. I cup Camille's jaw and kiss her again, deepening the intensity of our lip-lock. I push the thought that it's her first time to the back of my mind. Although it bears a certain significance, I can't focus on it too much. Because this is a kind of first for me as well. This moment is saying a lot of things about me as well.

During the last few years of our relationship, Rebecca kept accusing me of no longer having any passion for her. I always denied it because I didn't experience it that way. But right now, as I'm sitting here kissing Camille, all the neurons in my brain firing simultaneously in a frenzy of building lust, I have to admit that if this is passion, these sensations running through me at this very moment, then Rebecca was right. I did not have any more passion for her.

Camille brings her hands to my jaw and our lips keep meeting and we've become this intertwined entity of fingers and skin and lips and tongues. When we catch our breath, she runs a finger over my lips. She doesn't say anything, just looks into my eyes as her finger skates along my lips, denting them.

"*Tu es si belle,*" she whispers.

I don't understand what it means but I automatically take it as a compliment. When she speaks French, her voice sounds different. More confident. More her, even though I don't know her at all. It sounds much more sensual than anything she says in English, and I feel something pulsing between my legs. A very ignored body part is reminding me of its presence.

The tip of Camille's finger slips into my mouth. She comes across so self-assured. Is this really her first time? Perhaps, when you wait long enough, the desire becomes so ingrained within your person that actions just happen, hands know what to do instinctively—like right now, she's pushing her finger lightly into my mouth. I suck on it and it's a new sensation that thrills me. I want to feel more of her. Her skin on mine. The weight of her body pressing into me.

She removes her finger from my mouth and I start pushing her down onto the couch. Camille suddenly looks so

HARPER BLISS

vulnerable on her back like that, looking up at me, her hair fanned out around her face. She looks less composed. More insecure. But I've got this. My instincts, though oft neglected, are quickly coming back to me. The couch is wide enough for me to lie next to her on my side, gluing myself to her, gazing down at her.

I run the back of my fingers along her cheek. How did this even happen? Was it only this morning that I stood in this very apartment, making a fool of myself in front of my temporary tenant? Did my subconscious already know that something was brewing? Is that when the heat started building in my veins? A heat that is now ready to explode out of me, take over completely. I'm consumed by the desire to give Camille pleasure. To let her know how it can be with a woman. Soft and intense and utterly satisfying. This wave of lust we've decided to ride is crashing over me. It's about to drown me in its force. I drag my finger along her jaw and between her collar bones, straight into her cleavage.

The thrill of discovery is unmistakable. Camille is much slighter than Rebecca. Her skin so pale. Her bones so fine.

"I want you," I say, the words getting half-stuck in the back of my throat. "So, so much."

"You have me." The smile she sends me is sensual and knowing, though I have no idea what she might actually know. Because, in this moment and in this situation, there's not much more to know than what is happening right now. There is no future. Our pasts don't matter. It's just now.

While I slip a hand inside her blouse and, in one swift motion, inside her bra cup, I lean down to kiss her.

When I feel her nipple between two fingers and press down with the lightest amount of force, she groans into my mouth.

I might be lying half on top of her, but it doesn't mean I feel in control of this situation. Should I ask her what she likes? Does she even know? *Just let it all go*, I remind myself. *Be in the moment*. I intensify the pressure of my lips on hers and

32

my fingers on her nipple. She squirms against me and I relish every second of it.

When we break from this kiss, I'm overcome with the urge to see her naked. My subconscious desire, of which I'm now sure it was there all along, is catching up with me, steering me. It has lost patience. I retract my hand from her warm breast and start unbuttoning her blouse. I push the sides away and drink in the sight of her. She has three freckles underneath her left breast and I connect them in an invisible line with my fingertip. I bow down and kiss her just above the belly button. The touch of my lips on her skin there sends a shiver up my spine.

Her own hand gets busy and finds a way inside my top from my neck down. It reaches the back of my bra and starts fumbling. I can only conclude that her impatience matches mine. She has been waiting a long time for this. So have I. To feel this alive again, this overtaken by lust.

"Maybe we should go into the bedroom," she says, when our eyes meet next.

I chuckle, then nod. "Let's go." I maneuver myself out of the couch and take her hand in mine. We rush into the bedroom, where the bed is pristinely made. Camille pulls the covers off unceremoniously, then stands in front of me.

"This might be easier from this angle." She slides her hands underneath my top and has my bra unhooked in a matter of seconds.

I follow her example and we keep undressing, taking off items of our own clothing while disrobing the other. It's as functional as it is sensual, because by the time I stand in front of her in just my panties, my pulse has picked up speed and the throbbing between my legs has intensified.

We slide into bed, end up lying on our sides, facing each other.

"Now what?" she asks.

Her question takes me aback. "Er…" I know what to do, just not really how to put it into words.

"I'm just joking," she says, and shuffles closer. "I know what I want." She brings her mouth to my ear. "You," she whispers.

Her words are just as enticing as when she slipped the tip of her finger into my mouth. We kiss again, but this time our almost-naked bodies press against each other. Her hard nipples push into the soft flesh of my breasts and her belly is warm against mine. Our legs slip in between each other's and we become so tangled up in each other, there's no way of telling where one body begins and the other ends, but by the color of our skin.

When we catch our breath, she brings her hand to my mouth again and, this time, rubs two of her fingers along my bottom lip. She slips them inside my mouth and I suck on them eagerly. It's an intimate gesture that ignites my arousal even more.

"You look so hot like that," she says. She stares at me intently, taking in every last detail of my face.

She slides her fingers out of my mouth and, all wet, she runs them over my lip again, then down to my breast. By the time they reach my nipple, the wetness has gone cold, and her fingers leave my nipple unbearably tight.

"I want you," I whisper, because it's the only thought left in my mind. My brain is only ruled by lust, by desire for this exquisite creature who is torturing my nipple, even though she's barely touching it. I feel it everywhere. In every nerve ending, in every cell, despite knowing such a thing is not possible. But my logical mind stopped working the instant Camille took that wine glass out of my hand and told me she was going to kiss me. Because what is happening right now is not normal Zoya Das behavior. I have never jumped into bed with a woman I just met. Not once in my life. Now, as I lie here, and Camille's delicious fingers travel down, I have to ask myself why the hell not? What was I so scared of?

Camille's hands dip further down, her fingers only

lightly touching me, but they're having a devastating effect nonetheless. I start to realize that, near the end with Rebecca, it was never like this. It makes this tryst with Camille all the more exciting. A thought burrows its way forward in my brain: was this what it was like for Rebecca when she first cheated on me? Is this how it made her feel: so wanted, so central to someone else's joy? The answer can only be yes. Why else would she have stooped to such dishonest lows?

And I know I shouldn't think of Rebecca, but I also know it's impossible not to. She was the person who was everything to me for such a long time. The one my life revolved around. Is this all it takes to climb out of the massive crater of pain she pushed me into? Feeling like this with a woman who will only be in Australia for a few more days?

A woman whose fingers are dangerously close to my pubic area. I push down my panties and wriggle out of them as best I can. Her eyes are still on mine. Her gaze on me is intense and a little disconcerting, but also very hot in its demand. It tells me what she wants from me. I want the exact same thing. To be in this moment with her. To experience this extreme pleasure with another person, to no longer feel alone in our grief. In the relationship crimes that have been done to us.

Camille's fingers skate along my pussy lips, which respond by throbbing and, though I have no way to verify, opening themselves up to her. My body is in control now. What did Rebecca call me one of the last times we had sex? Uptight. Too in my head. My head has nothing to do with what is happening right now.

I look into Camille's eyes again. They seem a lighter brown in here. Her pupils grow wider as the tip of her finger enters me. A glimmer of a smile plays on her lips. It reaches her eyes. And I give myself up to her. I meet her thrust, which is very light and gentle. Like she's discovering me. She is. And herself as well.

"More," I urge, because my desire seems to have found a direct connection to my tongue. I never asked Rebecca for more. Maybe I should have. Maybe things would have been different if I had. Maybe I wouldn't be enjoying the hands of a stranger on me in my rental flat.

Camille fucks me harder. My eyes have fallen shut, but when I open them for an instant, I see she is still looking at me. This must be the first time she's seeing a woman enveloped in such rapture. The first time she's the source of it. To mean this very thing to someone is an honor.

I give myself up to her more, because what we're doing right now is a gift to both of us. It's the pair of us saying yes to the rest of our lives. To stepping away from the mistakes and pain of the past. This is the moment when we choose the future. When looking back is still an option but no longer one we want to indulge in.

As good as her fingers feel inside of me, they won't be enough. I'm not a stickler for reaching orgasm every time I have sex—another thing that used to drive Rebecca crazy—but this time, it feels like an absolute necessity. As though the experience wouldn't be complete without me breaking free from this plateau and coming at Camille's divine hands. All of this needs to happen on instinct, because it's our instinct that has brought us here. It isn't days and weeks we've spent in each other's company, getting to know each other better, learning intimate details about each other. This is another kind of thrill. And as thrilling as the unknown and unfamiliar is at this moment—the different angle with which her fingers penetrate me and the undoing sensation of her gaze on me at all times—it's not going to be enough to unleash the climax that is building beneath my flesh.

I open my eyes and look at her. I take in the intensity of her facial expression for a split second, just because it's such a turn-on. Her brow is furrowed in concentration; her lips are pursed together. She has the loveliest pout I've seen on a woman.

"Lick me," I say. "Lick my clit." I'm not usually one to say such words aloud, and to hear them said in my own voice is surprisingly arousing. I give her a quick, encouraging nod of the head.

She nods back, then starts retracting her fingers.

I bring my hand to her arm and she looks up at me. "Leave those."

She sinks her teeth into her bottom lip and blinks. I think she gets the picture, because the next moment, she hunches between my legs. Her fingers keep delving deep and I already feel her breath on my clit. It's almost enough to push me over the edge. Another surprise.

Then her tongue lands on my swollen clit. Tentatively at first, exploring again. As soon as she finds something resembling a rhythm of circling her tongue around and over it, it does all become too much for me. I lose myself to her touch and let go. I picture her face. I can still recall every tiniest feature. The thin lines of her eyebrows. The dimple in her cheek even when she isn't smiling. The lock of hair that falls across her forehead. The utter deliciousness of her French accent. The way she said she'd never been with a woman before. Her tongue. Her fingers. The emotions of this entire day come crashing down on me and transform into something else entirely. A release so great I find myself clasping the back of her head in my hands, holding on to something as the tingling heat spreads through me and reaches my extremities in record time.

I let out a high-pitched moan, filling the rooms of this apartment, which I was cursing this very morning—oh, the irony of that. This is all thanks to batteries and how they always die.

"Oh, god. Oh," I moan as I try to indicate to Camille that I've had enough, that my body can't take anymore. My muscles are relaxed, my limbs lazy, my lips spread into their widest smile.

She crawls up to me. Her smile matches mine.

"*Mon dieu,*" she says. I don't need to know a lot of French to know what that means.

She brings her fingers in between our faces and looks at them intently. Her smile fades, then deepens. She spreads her fingers and traces them over my lips. I smell myself on her, then taste myself as she slips them inside my mouth again. While her fingers are in my mouth she kisses me on the lips. As though she can't get enough of me. Maybe she can't. The thought fills me with lust again. Depletion of desire is no option in this bedroom. Not with Camille lying half on top of me and thrusting fingers into my mouth. How long before she goes? No, I shouldn't think about that. The night is only half over. We have time. I haven't had my wicked way with her. A desire so great, I push her off me and assert myself on top of her.

She looks up at me doe-eyed, as if she can't quite believe what just happened and what is about to happen next. There are so many ways in which I want her. So many images of Camille all over me, and me all over her, run through my mind, but I think it better to keep things simple for her first time. To bestow upon her the simple but deep pleasure of a woman bowing down between her legs with the sole intent of making all the lust that's been building inside of her explode. I don't ask her what she likes. I'll find out as I go along.

I kiss her, our lips spreading wide from the get-go, letting as much of each other in as possible. Her hands are in my hair. Her breasts are soft against mine. I can feel her wetness on my knee, soaking through her panties.

I'm overcome by the acute desire to get the last piece of fabric off her. The last barrier between my tongue and her sex. I kiss a quick path down, then settle between her legs. I gauge the fabric of her underwear. It's black and sheer and I don't have the patience to take them off her delicately. I hook my fingers underneath the waistband and yank them down. They stop halfway down her legs. I pull again to get them off completely, and hear the noise of tearing fabric and I see the panties have come apart at the seam.

I look up at her. What must she think of this madwoman sitting between her legs. Perhaps she'll never rent an Airbnb again. But a smile plays on her lips. Her eyes have narrowed. It seems to me that my little display of brute power turned her on. All I wanted to convey was exactly how much I want her. Enough to rip apart a fine piece of French lingerie.

I glance down at the glistening wetness in front of me. I can't wait any longer. I need to taste her, have her all over my face, ravage her. I bow down to her and let my tongue touch down softly.

CHAPTER SIX

I wake to a finger caressing my skin. Then lips press against my shoulder. Before I even open my eyes, I break into a smile. Camille. My gorgeous Frenchwoman. Can it be more dramatically romantic? Being swept away by a tall, dirty-blonde stranger with a French accent. Because that's what she did. She swept me right off my feet.

"*Bonjour,*" she says, her finger now stroking my cheek.

"Hey." I open my eyes. I want to lie here like this for a little while longer. Just look at her. How the morning sunlight catches in her hair, makes her eyes shine. Bask in last night's glory for as long as I can. I'm going to have to call Caitlin later today—if I can ever wrestle myself away from Camille long enough to do so—and tell her she was right. This was exactly the kind of distraction I needed.

"Did you sleep well?" Camille's accent is more pronounced upon waking. It makes her sound all the more endearing.

"Hm-mm," I hum. I suppress the urge to kiss her, even though it's strong and seems to be overtaking me quickly as I awaken more. I have no idea what the one-night stand protocol is. Do I leave and wash her scent off me at home? Do we have breakfast together? It's Saturday. I'll just go with the flow.

"What are you doing today?" she asks.

My heart skips a beat. I need to think for a minute. Whatever plans I made for today seem to have slipped my mind completely. I rack my brain and remember. "I have a yoga class scheduled this afternoon and I was going to see the new Malick movie with my friend Jason tonight."

"Oh." Is that a shadow of disappointment crossing her face?

"Did you, er, want to do something together?"

"I don't want to mess up your plans." She clears her throat. "I also understand if this has to be goodbye. If it makes it easier."

"I don't want that. I'd like to see you again. When do you leave exactly?"

"My plane takes off at eleven thirty on Thursday morning."

"That gives us five days."

"Oceans of time." Camille scoots closer.

"I'll cancel yoga. You can either join me and Jason for the movie, or I can brush him off. If I tell him it's for a woman, he won't mind at all."

"Won't he, now? What will you tell him?"

"That I met a woman named Camille who gave me a whole new perspective on my sad life."

"And I thought we French were dramatic."

"You should meet my family. Indians take drama to a whole new level."

"As much as I'd love to, let's wait a while for family introductions." Camille chuckles.

"Oh, no. I didn't mean—"

"I know." Her hands are on my belly. "I'm just joking." She kisses my shoulder, then finds my gaze again. "Let's make the most of the five days we have left."

———

I take a deep breath before we enter the Pink Bean. We could have gone to breakfast somewhere else, but Camille said she enjoyed the croissants the day before—and I wouldn't live it down if Caitlin, Sheryl or Micky saw me having breakfast with Camille somewhere else. They'd accuse me of trying to hide something—or find other allegations to throw at me, no doubt.

"I'm starving," Camille says. "Must have worked up quite an appetite." She slips her arm through mine as we line up at the counter.

I go a bit soft on the inside at her touch—and her words. Thankfully, there's no one here that I know. Not yet, anyway. It's not my habit to spend Saturday morning in Darlinghurst and I don't know what everyone else's are. I do know that neither Micky nor Josephine work here on the weekend.

We order pastries, coffee, and fresh orange juice and find a table in the farthest corner from the door. I've already canceled my yoga class. Camille insisted I'd keep my rendezvous with Jason tonight. She can always get her own ticket for the movie if she can't bear to be away from me by then—her own words. But I'll probably cancel anyway.

"You should see Sydney," I say once we've sat down.

She shakes her head. "I'm seeing all of Sydney I want to see right now."

"That's not what I mean. God knows when and if you'll ever be back. There's a lot to see."

"The Opera House, the Harbour Bridge, the fish market, Bondi beach... Yes, I've read all about it. Yet, I have no desire to see any of it with my own eyes. What I would like to see, however, is how Zoya Das lives." Her eyes are crinkled up in a smile.

"That can be arranged."

"Do you live far from here?" she asks.

My attention is snagged by a loud group of people entering the Pink Bean. I recognize Micky, Robin, and Micky's teenagers. They head straight for the counter and don't see me.

"Olivia had a craving for Kristin's sticky buns and arguing with a fifteen-year-old girl is very difficult on a Saturday morning," Micky says to the person behind the counter.

"Our moment of peace and quiet may be disturbed imminently," I say, knitting my brows together.

"I don't mind meeting your friends. A person's friends say so much about them."

"Says the person who sometimes hangs out with Dominique Laroche. Have you met her partner?"

Micky and company occupy one of the big tables in the middle of the shop. They still haven't seen us.

"I have met Stéphanie. Definitely the most unconventional first lady on the face of the earth. She's keeping a low profile. When I met her, we talked about her role in Dominique's public life, and she countered by asking if I had the faintest clue who Angela Merkel's husband was and his role in her life." She chuckles. "I had to admit I didn't."

"That might be true, but I imagine the interest in Merkel's husband is far less than in Laroche's much younger lesbian lover. It's human nature. I have no desire to know anything about some bland guy, but my ears always perk up when I hear something about Stéphanie Mathis. I just can't help myself."

"You're a lesbian. You're more attuned to news about your kind."

"Trust me, it's not only among lesbians. What's it like in France? It must be hard for her."

Camille shakes her head. "It's not. We are a nation who, historically, don't care what our leaders do in the bedroom. We are truly not interested. We always have far more fascinating things to talk about. Although when Dominique first came out, a shock wave did travel through the country. But in the end, once things have settled down, what does it truly matter who the president is with?"

"She's France's first female president. That's far more important."

"And she's progressive. At least on things that matter to

me. That's what's most important to me," Camille says.

From the corner of my eye, I see Micky's son has clocked me. The first time I went to Micky's house and he was there, he flushed so red I thought his skin would remain that color forever. The entire table turns to me now. I give them a sheepish wave.

"Here we go," I say.

"I look forward to it." Camille shoots me a confident smile. It makes her look so utterly gorgeous, I want to just leave the Pink Bean and go back to the apartment. I want to do all day what we did last night. Repeat performance after repeat performance. Goodness, she's beautiful.

"Morning," Micky says a bit too chirpily. She holds a hand out to Camille. "I didn't get a chance to introduce myself properly yesterday. I'm Micky. I work here on weekdays." She points her thumb behind her. "That's my family over there."

Camille gives her a very charming smile while taking Micky's hand in hers. "Very nice to meet you, Micky."

"Chris is about to faint again," she says to me. "He has a huge crush on Zoya," she adds as an aside to Camille. "But it's better than him having a crush on my girlfriend, I guess. Which I believe he had when I first introduced them." She rolls her eyes. "Teenagers and their hormones."

"Oh, I know all about that. I have a nineteen-year-old son," Camille says.

It makes me realize we've barely talked about her children and her life back home.

"All I can say is, don't ever show him a picture of Zoya Das," Micky jokes.

"I won't." Camille winks at me.

"I'll leave you to it," Micky says and—thankfully—saunters back to her family.

"Guess who was still in the closet less than a year ago after divorcing her husband?" I say.

"It seems to be a very common occurrence all around

the globe."

I nod. "When I first came out, you would not believe how much mail I got from women who were in Micky's—and your—situation. Women feeling trapped in their marriage. Not knowing how to break free from a choice they made decades ago. More often than not, children are involved, complicating it all so much more."

"And look at Micky now," Camille says and glances over at Micky's table.

"According to Josephine, she's *obnoxiously* happy now."

"I'm pretty happy right now." Camille tilts her head. "As long as I get to spend the day with you."

"That can easily be arranged. I can even make it so I don't have anything to do tomorrow either."

"Really?" Camille's voice grows husky.

"But I insist on showing you at least some of the sights."

Camille nods. "I can't possibly have you ripping up more of my panties."

I chuckle. "I'll buy you some new ones today."

"Maybe not too high-quality ones."

"Good morning." Caitlin's voice startles me. I was so wrapped up in looking into Camille's eyes I didn't even see Caitlin come in. "You must be Camille." Caitlin grins at Camille. "Caitlin James. Pleasure to meet you."

Emotions war inside of me. On the one hand, I think Camille and I should get out of here as quickly as possible, before Sheryl and Kristin come down, followed by Amber and Martha hopping in for some tea. On the other hand, I want to say to Caitlin: "You see. I can do this." Although it would just make her feel smug. Or perhaps just happy for me. Caitlin's return to Australia coincided with my break-up from Rebecca, which has been a great help to me. Because of her, I had an outside perspective on all the matters that drove Rebecca and me apart. And she introduced me to a bunch of people who don't remind me of the life I used to have.

People who don't have to walk on egg shells around me and worry about a slip of the tongue, accidentally mentioning they spent time with Rebecca and Julie.

"I'm surprised you know my name." Camille says it with a smile in her voice.

"Let's just say I was there when you texted Zoya and I was the one to push her in the right direction." Caitlin winks at me. "Call me later," she says.

"You do know a lot of the customers here." Camille sits there grinning. "Seems to me your problem is not being recognized by strangers at all. It's being left alone by your friends while you're having breakfast with last night's conquest."

"Oh, no. You were absolutely not a *conquest* to me."

That smile again. "Seems like the French have a decidedly different sense of humor than the Australians."

"Touché." I drink my coffee while I consider my next words carefully. "Do we, er need to talk about what this is?"

Her face darkens. "It can only be one thing. I think we should at least be clear about that."

"I know."

"But let's enjoy the weekend. I'd much rather spend my last one in this gorgeous country with an equally gorgeous woman by my side."

"You got it." I send her a smile, even though, on the inside, it feels a little bitter sweet. "Let's get out of here, though. I don't want any more interruptions."

"Deal." Camille makes quick work of her coffee and croissant, and so do I.

CHAPTER SEVEN

"Benoit is nineteen and Florence is twenty-five," Camille says. I've taken her to a quiet beach tourists haven't annexed yet, especially this time of year. We're strolling along the shoreline and, apart from the plans we've made to go back to my place later, I don't want this walk to end. I want to listen to Camille's voice for days on end. I want this weekend to be everlasting. Argh. I need to remind myself this is just a prolonged one-night stand.

"Ben's in his first year of university in Marseille, so I don't see him that often. It was a big change when he left home. Definitely some of that—what do you call it?—empty nest thing going on. Luckily Flo lives in Paris so I get to see her a lot. And soon I will become a free babysitter to my granddaughter." Her voice softens.

"Twenty-five seems so young to become a mother these days," I say.

"Believe me, I told her the exact same thing. For some reason, it's her dream to have a big family. It can't possibly have been the harmonious family life Jean-Claude and I gave her. But it's what she wants. These days, kids want it all. Even though she's hardly a child anymore. A career. A thriving marriage. A bunch of children. Frankly, I don't see how all of that is possible at the same time. But she believes in it with such vigor. She takes after her father in that respect. He has always gone after what he wants with a conviction I often thought admirable. These days I tend to wonder at what cost." She takes my hand in hers and an arrow of heat shudders through me. "I started planning this trip as soon as I found out Flo was pregnant. It was now or never. I can't imagine traveling this far and for this long once that girl is born. At least not for a while, anyway. The timing was exactly right: Ben at university, me home alone, Flo and Mathieu expecting. And here I am."

"At the very end of your journey." I hold onto her hand a little tighter.

"But what an ending it is." She squeezes back with strong fingers. "Have you ever wanted children?" she asks.

I take a moment to think about this. It's been so long since I had a conversation about having children. "Before I was with Rebecca, I was alone for a few years. I thought about it a couple of times then. Most of my lesbian friends who had children had them from a previous heterosexual relationship. I know things have changed a lot in the past decade and a half, but back when I was questioning whether I wanted kids or not, times were different. I'm not saying it's easy now. And far from cheap either. But back in the day—when it was my time, so to speak—it seemed too much of an impossibility. And I guess my maternal instincts never developed that much. I never had that ache I've heard some women talk about. Like their life could not possibly be complete if they didn't have a child. I think I'm just part of the strain of genes who don't feel their life is a failure because they haven't procreated. And who knows, if my circumstances had been different, or if Rebecca had really wanted children, but it wasn't the case, so…"

"I was a year younger than Flo is now when I had her, so suffice it to say I never gave it much thought. It was just how things were. I'm racking my brain trying to think of someone I know from my generation who didn't have children."

"It just goes to show the implicit demands society makes of us. Most people never question the status quo."

"They just breed." Camille bumps her arm into mine.

She's so easy to talk to. Not just flirt with, but have an actual conversation with. It gives me an idea.

"This is completely off topic…"

"That's fine." She stops and pulls me toward her. "I love a good meandering conversation. That's how you find out the most."

"That's what I wanted to talk to you about." This is just a hunch, a fleeting thought I probably shouldn't have paid attention to. "You know what I do for a living."

"Yes. Which reminds me. Is there a way I can download all of your shows and put them on my laptop so I can watch them on the plane?"

My lips break into a spontaneous smile again. "My show isn't really about me. My role is to fade into the background and let others shine."

"For the life of me, I can't imagine you fading into any background."

"You're such a flatterer." I throw my arms around her neck. The day is chilly and I'm glad to feel Camille's body near.

"What did you want to ask me?" She nuzzles my neck with her nose.

"I'd like to interview you as I do with the guests on my show. And record it." I intensify the clasp of my arms around her neck. "I don't think I can just let you go without a lasting memory. I mean, I probably could, but I don't want to. Why should I?"

"Didn't you say you and your team research guests for a long time before you interview them?" Camille asks.

"This would be a different kind of interview. More exploratory than usual."

"I've seen a few clips. The one in which you interview Ruby Rose is very popular on YouTube apparently. Must have been because of the sexual tension."

I shake my head. "People will always see what they want

to see."

"Just so you know, if *we* do this, the sexual tension will be palpable on the screen…" She bites my earlobe. "So I have a counter offer."

"I'm all ears," I whisper, which causes her to sink her teeth into my earlobe again.

"You can interview me all you want if, afterward, I can make a video of my own."

"What kind of video did you have in mind?" If I'm catching her drift, the thought is at the same time exhilarating and terrifying.

"You and me in the bedroom." Her lips are on my neck, touching.

"A sex tape?" I blurt out.

"If that's what you want to call it."

I chuckle. "I'm not so sure of that. I'm not sure it's wise."

"I never said it would be wise." She pushes herself away from me and stares at me. "It would be irresponsible and foolish, but oh so hot. And a lasting memory we can use over and over again."

"When you put it like that…" I pull her close again. She could convince me of everything in a heartbeat, but I can't help but be cautious. "Still, the possible negative consequences need thinking about."

"The only way there could ever possibly be negative consequences is if the video got leaked."

"Indeed. I mean, you're about to become a grandmother. Think about it."

"So, it comes down to a matter of trust," Camille says.

"Hm." I look away from her for an instant. "As you might have guessed, I have some trust issues."

"Hey." She takes a step so she can stand in front of me again. "You're not alone with those." A pause. "Maybe it can be a good exercise. For the both of us."

"But I barely—"

Camille brings a finger to my lips—she really does like to touch them—and says, "I know what you're going to say. You barely know me." She removes her finger and cups her hand around my jaw. "Sometimes it takes a stranger to restore our confidence and trust in humanity."

"That's all well and good, but it still doesn't mean we should make a sex tape."

Camille's face is so open, her eyes so disarming and friendly. "True. So, let's sleep on it. We have a few more days before I leave. Let's see how you feel about it on my last day." She leans in and kisses me fully on the lips, one hand slipping right under my jacket and blouse. "And I hope you know what I mean by sleep," she says when we break from the kiss. "Shall we continue our walk?"

I nod, take her hand in mine, which feels like a surprisingly natural gesture, and stare out into the sea for a few minutes as we walk.

"I've been lied to and cheated on for the better part of twenty years. My husband had a mistress when I was in hospital after giving birth to our second child," Camille says. "But I had no choice but to put my trust in people again. What kind of life would I have if I didn't?"

I inhale a large gulp of sea air. "You seem like such a confident, well-rounded woman. How did you manage to stay married to him for such a long time?"

"Because he was the father of my children." She falls silent. "I know how it makes me look. Like a weak woman who didn't have the strength to walk away from a failed marriage. I had to face myself in the mirror asking myself that question every day, until I reached the conclusion that marriage is about so much more than fidelity." Her breath shudders. "I didn't want to raise my children alone. That was a choice I made early on and I stuck with it. Also, because I wasn't ready to come out, I guess. Not for a long time. And I knew it was futile to demand of Jean-Claude he stop messing around with other women. It's only natural for us mere mortals to be attracted to more people than the one we've chosen to marry. I fully believe in that. Some people choose to act on that attraction. For some, like my ex-husband, it's more like a compulsion. In the end, it mattered less to me than having to make a life on my own. And I know I did say last night that I took my marriage vows too seriously to take things further with a woman I met… But that wasn't entirely truthful. I was scared. Scared of what it might do to me. Of the point of no return. In that respect, I have always valued my role as a mother more than any other role I've had in my life. Which is one of the reasons I came on this trip after my youngest left home. And why I could finally push for a divorce when Ben was in his last year of high school."

"Wow."

"And I wish my story was unusual," Camille continues, "but it's not. It's as commonplace as anything. So many women have done what I've done, because we are mothers and our children always come first."

"It reminds me a lot of Micky's story, except I don't think Darren cheated on her."

"Oh, there are endless variations, but it always comes down to the same thing."

"What about the lack of respect your husband showed you by going behind your back time and time again?"

"He showed his respect for me in other ways and I had to learn not to let my respect for him depend on that. Let me be clear here, for Jean-Claude it was definitely compulsive. Things could have been so different between us if only he'd been honest. We could have had a productive conversation, come to some sort of arrangement. But that was not the case."

"Like an open marriage, you mean?" I chuckle. "You should talk to Caitlin."

"Is she an expert on the matter?" Camille's voice is serious.

"Oh yes. Something she and I disagree on greatly."

"Really? Have you always disagreed on it? Or only since you found out you'd been cheated on?"

Camille should be the interviewer. She always has the best questions. "She lived in America for a long time and came back just as things went awry between me and Rebecca, so I guess my vision on the matter was a little tainted in most conversations we've had about it. But, yes, I do know that cheating and dishonesty have no place in an open relationship. It's about the exact opposite. I know all the theories, I just don't think I would be able to live like that." My tone is getting tenser. I can so easily predict this conversation spiraling into a rant about Rebecca—the last topic I want to discuss with Camille on this beautiful autumn day.

"I would love to talk to Caitlin some time," Camille says.

"I'm sure she would love to talk to you." I run my thumb over the palm of her hand. "Would you like me to set something up?"

"That would be nice. Just to get a different perspective on you."

"It's so unfair. I don't get to chat to any of your friends."

"You would have to travel to Paris for that."

"Only if you can hook me up with Dominique Laroche."

"I'll see what I can do," she says, stops in her tracks, and kisses me again. To anyone passing by, we must look like a couple newly in love.

"How about we go back to my place now?" I ask.

———

"Did our conversation from earlier upset you?" Camille asks after I've given her a quick tour of my house—technically still my and Rebecca's house. It feels strange to bring Camille here, where we lived together for more than ten years. When I asked Rebecca if she'd ever brought Julie here to have sex with and she reluctantly confirmed she had, it was one of the things that stung the most. Because it violated the place we had created together, out of our love and commitment to each other. Another reason I want to get rid of this house as quickly as possible.

"No. Not really. It just made me think of my ex and, er, some of the things she accused me of."

"If there's one thing I've learned it's that exes are very good at blaming others for their own mistakes, to justify them. But it cuts both ways. When a relationship ends, it's hardly ever because one person screwed up. I think it might be statistically impossible. And I'm a scientist. I know all about statistics."

"How did you possibly screw up in your marriage?"

"In many ways I don't really want to confess to you right now. It doesn't really strike me as the right timing." She heels off her shoes and draws her feet up onto the couch.

"Well, then…" I know this question is completely beside the point. I just feel like some mischief to lighten the mood. "Do tell me if you also think I lack passion."

Camille gives a throaty laugh. "From my point of view, passion is the very last thing you lack."

"Thank you." I know I'm comparing apples to oranges, but it doesn't matter. I just wanted to hear Camille say it.

"Speaking of *passion*." She pronounces it the French way, and it sounds so much more sensual. It makes me want to enroll in an immersive French course as soon as I get the chance. "Or maybe I should call it chemistry. Or attraction. I sincerely believe it's a thing that exists in a tangible way between two people. Like last night, there was quite a bit of it in the air." She extends her leg so her foot touches my thigh. "I wouldn't mind another taste of that. Even if just to see if it's still there. As I just said, I'm a scientist and I like to do research experiments."

"What kind of experiment did you have in mind?" Something in my core is melting already. It's her eyes on me and how they take me back to last night, and the change of light in them and how it states her intentions.

"Well, basically, my second time with a woman." Her smile is less confident.

"For a first timer, you were pretty spectacular." I grab hold of her leg and stretch it over my lap, massaging her calf through her jeans.

She scrunches her lips into a pout. "Then we must test to see if it wasn't beginner's luck."

"Oh, luck was definitely involved. If those smoke detector batteries hadn't died, we would never have met."

"Yeah, that's what I was thinking throughout that sleepless night every time that annoying beep woke me up. I'm about to encounter an incredible stroke of luck. It's what kept me going." She brings her hand to her neck. "I so want to ask you about your first time, but my mind is too preoccupied right now." She sucks her lip into her mouth.

"How about I tell you all about it later? After the experiment?"

"Hm-mm." Camille bends her legs, pushes herself up, and is on top of me in a matter of seconds.

CHAPTER EIGHT

"Are you a woman of leisure now?" Caitlin asks.

"No. I'm about to head to the office. I was just dropping Camille off at the apartment. I need a strong coffee before I start my work day."

"I waited for your call all weekend, but none came." She winks at Josephine behind the counter.

"I was otherwise engaged."

"I bet you were."

"What did you do yesterday?" Josephine asks.

"I showed her around Sydney."

"Mainly the area around Balmain, I suspect," Caitlin says.

"Here you go. With an extra shot." Josephine hands me my tall black coffee.

"I'm too tired to play coy." I glance at the smug smile on Caitlin's face. "I wish I had the kind of job where I could just call in sick. I was up half the night with Camille and every second of it was utterly glorious."

"You are stretching the concept of a one-night stand to its limits," Caitlin says.

"I know, but she's leaving in three days. Speaking of." I sip from the coffee, in desperate need of a hit of caffeine. "Would you two like to have dinner with us?"

Caitlin brings a hand to her chest. "Such an honor to bestow upon the modest non-French likes of us."

Josephine shakes her head. "Don't mind her, Zoya. We'd

love to. I'm free tomorrow night."

"That works for me," Caitlin says. "You're buying, though. You owe me for making that magical booking for you and Camille."

"It's a date then."

"And don't worry." Caitlin's Monday morning energy is enviable and enervating at the same time. "We won't waste too much of your time."

"Morning." Sheryl has approached us. When she sees me she quirks up her eyebrows. "Someone's had an interesting weekend, I hear."

"Honestly, for a bunch of grown women, news travels way too fast around here. You'd think this was a place where gossip comes to thrive instead of a place to enjoy coffee."

"Ooh, defensive," Caitlin says.

"I ran into Micky this weekend," Sheryl says. "She told me."

"It wasn't me who spilled the beans," Caitlin says. "I would never."

"Where is Micky this morning?" I ask. Even though I'm glad for one less inquiring mind that wants to know too much.

"She has the day off," Josephine says.

"When is, er, she leaving?" Sheryl asks me.

"Camille is leaving on Thursday morning." Oh, just saying her name to my friends. "Her plane takes off at eleven thirty in the morning." I should plan a really exciting activity for that day. Thursdays are always recording days so I definitely won't be able to take time off to accompany Camille to the airport. It's simply not possible. Who am I interviewing again this week? My mind is so preoccupied, the interviewee's name escapes me.

"So, it's a holiday romance," Sheryl says.

"It is for her because she's on holiday. It's back to the dreariness of everyday life for me after she's gone."

"Aren't we being a touch dramatic?" Caitlin asks.

How can I explain to her that a woman I met only three days ago has already shifted my perspective on everything. That I dread this coming Thursday when she will fly out of my life for good. When I will come home in the evening to the same old house Rebecca and I shared and everything will be covered in a new layer of gloom. A double one. One post-Rebecca. And one post-Camille. And how the upcoming loss of an overly long one-night stand is going to hurt me just as much as the unraveling of a sixteen-year relationship. That I know it was meant to do me good. Make me feel desirable and alive and get me out of my own head where I was spinning circles feeling sorry for myself. And that I fear it will only end up increasing my self-pity. Because the madness of it all is that, after these three short, romantic, frenzied days, I don't want Camille to leave. I want to talk to her more about all the things she's so eloquent about. I want to marvel at the way she articulates her thoughts, and how her cheek dimple deepens when she ponders a question for a minute and holds up a finger, and says, "I'm still thinking" and the *th* always sounds more like an *s*.

I shrug. "I'd best get to work."

"We're here if you want to talk," Sheryl says. "You know that, don't you?"

"I might move into the rental after she leaves. Be closer to my new friends." It may sound like a joke, but I should just do it.

"Josephine is singing here on Friday," Caitlin says. "We'll make a weekend of it. We can go look at houses."

"Thanks."

"We'll see you tomorrow." Josephine steps from behind the counter and throws her arms around me. "And every day after that if you need to," she whispers in my ear.

CHAPTER NINE

I have the kind of job that doesn't allow me to daydream too much. My team of researchers are constantly throwing new information at me that I need to parse and evaluate to see if I could base a good question on it. But throughout the day, I can't stop thinking about the questions I would ask Camille. The ones that would really lay her bare to me. Over the weekend, I've asked her many a question already, but often her answer was drowned out by a new onslaught of passion —and experiments that needed to be repeated over and over again.

Every time I think of our possible recorded interview, my mind wanders to what *she* asked to record. What she wants to take home as a reminder. And what it means that she asked me at all. The thought of recording ourselves while having sex excites me, there's no doubt. Then my mind gets lost in another tailspin of delving up memories of the weekend.

"Well, well, well." Jason sticks his head around the door of my office. "Let me have a look. Ah yes, dark circles under the eyes but an unmistakable glint of satisfaction in them. Okay, it was worth being stood up for." He shoots me a big, toothy grin.

"I'll make it up to you, Jase. I'll have all the time in the world as of Thursday." I hate that, suddenly, now that the weekend has ended, everything seems to have become a reminder of Camille leaving. I will make a point of not having it overshadow the time we have left. We are grown women, not love-sick teenagers involved in a summer fling.

She'll go; I'll forget about her; move on.

"I'm counting on it. And a full blow-by-blow as well." He sits down in one of the chairs. "Though do give me a little something to whet my appetite already."

I tell him about the batteries, the dreadful meeting with Rebecca, and the forty-eight hours of sheer bliss that followed with Camille after.

"Here's the best I can do for you," he says, putting on his semi-serious TV face. "I can falsely predict extremely inclement weather passing through for twenty-four hours as of Thursday morning, keeping all international flights on the ground for at least a day."

"I wouldn't want you to violate the weathermen code of ethics just so I can have a few more orgasms, but thanks anyway." I have to chuckle.

"Looks to me like we're talking about a bit more than a few orgasms here, Zo."

"Is it that obvious?"

"Hm, kind of," he says.

"But it's so stupid."

He waggles his finger in front of me. "Oh no, it most certainly is not."

"Even if it's not stupid, it's still impossible."

"Nothing is impossible, just untried." He uses his serious television voice.

"I can't stop thinking about her." I bring my hands to my head. "If only she was from New Zealand, or some godforsaken settlement in the Northern Territory, but not Paris. That's too far. You know how long the journey is from Sydney to Paris? Twenty-four hours! And that's the best-case scenario."

"But surely the fact that she's from Paris adds to her attraction."

I sigh. "Oh god, yes."

"You can't have one without the other." He drums his fingertips on my desk. "Hey, don't worry. In between forecasting the weather, I will dedicate all my waking hours to concocting a plan to make you forget about her as quickly as possible. If"—he holds up his finger again—"that's what you want."

"Ask me again in a few days."

He shuffles his chair closer. "Just so you know, these things happen all the time. People fall in love with other people who live on the other side of the world all the time. If it's meant to be, it's meant to be."

"I'm not falling in love, okay. That's a bit too... I don't know. Inaccurate. Perhaps I'm falling in lust. Well yes, I've definitely done that. But love? That's just ridiculous."

"I said *in* love."

"What's the difference? Please, explain it to me, Jason."

"I don't think you need me to explain anything to you at all. You are one of the smartest people I know. And the hottest—for a woman. I don't even need to have met this Camille to know that she is pining for you right now."

If anything, Jason makes me laugh with his exaggerations. "She just sent me this." I show him a picture of Camille in front of the Opera House, pretending to sing.

"She's thinking of you at the very least."

"And I'm thinking of her." I expel another feeling-sorry-for-myself sigh. "Even if I were falling in love with her and we embarked on something long-distance and impossible, I'm the very first woman she's ever been with. She's not just going to sit around and wait until I go to Paris once a year. She'll want to explore."

"Have more of what you gave her a taste of." Jason breaks out into a sweet smile. "But you *have* thought about it."

"Ever since this morning, it seems to be all I can think about."

"Talk to her."

I shake my head. "No. There's no point. We both know what this is."

"But what if it's more than you're both willing to admit?"

"I met her on Friday morning, Jason. It can't possibly be any more."

"Let it be noted on the record that I strongly disagree." He leans over my desk. "Sometimes, in love, all it takes is one second. A flick of someone's lashes. A corner of the mouth curling up. Looking into a stranger's eyes at the exact right time."

"Yes, sure." I'm so very desperate to believe him. "If that stranger doesn't have a life and a family on the other side of the world."

"That's another matter. I'm just trying to make you see that you shouldn't feel silly because of your emotions, because of how she makes you feel."

Sean, my most junior researcher, knocks on the door, which is still open. This really isn't a conversation Jason and I should have at work, and especially not with the door open.

"Oh, sorry, boss," he says. "Hi, Jason. Something urgent just came in, but I can come back in a few."

"I was just leaving." Jason stands. He turns to me and mouths, "I'm right." At least that's what I think he's trying to say. I both wish and don't wish that he is.

After work, I drive straight to Darlinghurst. Traffic is dense and moves much too slowly for my taste. Don't these people know I have no time to waste? That a woman who is about to leave is waiting for me. I should have asked her to meet me at my house. The drive to work is much shorter. Maybe I should rethink my decision to move to Darlinghurst. I like the neighborhood, but I'm not interested in adding half an hour to my commute each way. Or maybe this standstill traffic is just a one-off. Just fate conspiring against me. Staying in Balmain and being reminded of Rebecca all the time isn't ideal either.

Every inch my car moves takes me closer to Camille. That thought keeps running through my head. It takes me to her— for now. As I look at my reflection in the rearview mirror, I wonder if it would have been better for me if I hadn't met her at all. Because attached to all the gloriousness of encountering someone like Camille—someone who ticks most, if not all, of my boxes—is also the wretchedness of having to let her go.

My phone starts ringing, pulling me right out of my doom and gloom. Camille's picture pops up on the screen. I activate the Bluetooth speaker and even before I say "Hello" my lips split into a wide smile.

"Where are you?" she asks. "I'm impatient."

"Thank goodness it's just that. I thought there was another emergency at the apartment."

"There is. Me. I'm your emergency." I love how she's willing to show it all, to not hold back because of the circumstances. Maybe it's because we have to compress an entire affair into a tiny number of days. It makes it more intense. Makes it feel like more than it would otherwise be.

"You are. Sadly, I'm stuck in traffic."

"Do you need me to entertain you?" Her voice sounds different over the phone. Deeper. More exotic.

"Yes, please. Tell me a story."

"Okay. Let me think for a minute." The silence that hangs in the car for the following seconds is almost unbearable.

"We can just talk." I manage to move my car forward a few more feet.

"No, no. You need to focus on traffic. I'll talk." She sounds bossy. Maybe it's her motherly voice. The one she used to tell her children off with when they were little. Before I left work, I couldn't resist googling her ex-husband Jean-Claude. A very handsome man, and not even in that off-kilter French way. I even found a few pictures of him and

President Laroche. All smiles and French elegance in tailor-made suits.

"So, once there were two women," Camille starts. "Who started what is now commonly referred to as an *Airbnb romance*. They met because of a technology that didn't exist a few years ago. This made them very modern. *Des femmes du monde, quoi.*"

I hate that my French is not that good. Why don't we get taught more of it in Australian schools? How we could benefit from being a bit worldlier. I want to understand every single word Camille speaks. Want to catch the meaning behind everything she says.

"These women both had some emotional baggage. Not to be confused with the luggage they brought into the Airbnb apartment, of course."

I burst into a giggle at her silly sense of humor. "Of course," I say.

"Shht. Focus on traffic," she says. "Let me tell my story."

Whatever was blocking the procession of cars I find myself in seems to have been cleared away, because I can pick up speed a little more. But now I just want to stay in the car until Camille has finished her story. I want to know how it ends.

"They were of a more mature age but very, er, well-kept. One of them was Australian, but of Indian descent."

My heart starts beating faster.

"She had the most expressive eyes. And her mouth. Oh, that mouth. Lips you'd want to kiss for days."

Oh Christ. I shouldn't feel like this when driving. Her words connect with something deep inside of me, making my pulse pick up speed as I accelerate.

"There are no two ways about it. The woman was beautiful and kind, albeit a bit, hm, how to put it, not very handy." Camille's voice remains serious. "Most of all, she was incredibly sexy. The kind of sexy that knocks you right over.

Not to be ignored. Unmistakable. Obviously, the other woman, who was French and visiting Australia and renting the Airbnb, had to do something. Because after she briefly met the Australian woman, she couldn't stop thinking about her. She was meant to be enjoying her last few days of relaxation and introspection and tourism, but instead, her mind was filled to the brim with thoughts of the Airbnb owner. It was stronger than herself. So she asked the other woman to go out and, miraculously, she said yes."

A pause. But I have no intention of saying anything. I should be in Darlinghurst in less than ten minutes, but now I don't want this drive to end. Although, no matter how much I'm enjoying this story, what lies at the end of this commute, will be far more divine. The Australian and French women will be joined at the hip—and quite a few other body parts— for the rest of the evening, throughout the night and most of the morning.

"They had a wonderful date under a bunch of fairy lights in this magical courtyard. It felt like it was all meant to be. Then..." She stops again. Maybe she's looking for words. Or just creating suspense. I wish I could see her while she's telling me this story. "Then, they made love. For the French woman, who was very new to all of this, it was like a fairy tale. Like magic. Kind of how she felt when she walked into the patio of that restaurant, into the magical atmosphere, not so much created by the decor or the lights, but by the woman she was there with. Because sometimes, maybe only once in your life, you meet someone, and it makes you feel something so... big. *Si incontournable.* That it made her feel as though everything was going to be all right in her life. If a thing like that can happen, just like that, in a flash, then other wonderful things will follow. There's just no other way."

My throat feels tight. Are those tears pricking behind my eyes?

"The two women spent an amazing weekend together. Talking. Getting to know each other better. Making love.

They made some memories they would never forget. But then the weekend ended. And the Australian woman had to get back to work, leaving the French woman alone all day. And what was strange was that this French woman had been traveling on her own, purposefully, for two months by then. She enjoyed the solitude, the room to breathe and think, but on the Monday after that weekend, she'd never felt so alone. Bereft almost, although she may have had a typical French flair for the dramatic. Lost. Like something important—no *the* most important part of her was missing. Even though she had to ask herself the question: how can it be? How is this possible?"

Camille goes silent for long seconds. I miss her voice reverberating through my car. Her funny inflections. Her endearing accent. Wait. Is this the end of the story?

"Zoya?" she asks, breaking her narrator character.

"Yes." My voice sounds so hollow and broken.

"We still have to come up with the ending for this story. Together."

"I'll be there in five minutes."

"Use them to think about how it will end," Camille says, and hangs up the phone quite abruptly.

This has been one of the most fascinating commutes of my life. I'm definitely moving to Darlinghurst. Maybe I can call Camille every day when I get back from work and she can tell me a story like that. Something to keep me going. What's the time difference again? But no, I shouldn't be thinking about that. I should be thinking about an ending for the story. A happy one. I rack my brain, but traffic gets busy around Darlinghurst and I need to find a place to park, and I know there's not really room for a happy ending here.

———

I knock on the door, my impatience coming through clearly in the intensity of my knock. I want to break down the door like I ripped off her panties the other day.

The door flies open and Camille stands in front of me.

It's like I haven't seen her in weeks instead of hours. She's freshly out of the shower and her hair is wet and falls heavily on her shoulders. She's barefoot and wrapped in a towel. She's so slight, it can wrap around her twice.

She drags me inside by the hand and slams the door shut behind me. She doesn't say anything, just pulls me closer, looks into my eyes, and kisses me. Her tongue invades my mouth from the get-go. Her wet hair slides across my face. Her hands pull me closer by the back of my head.

When we break apart, she looks at me, breathlessly, and says, "I can't remember ever feeling this way."

I lick my lips, buying time. What I say next will make a difference. But all I have is this question I've been dragging along with me all day. "What is happening to us?"

She shakes her head, sinks her teeth into her bottom lip the way she does. "We must be losing our minds."

"There's no better way to describe it." I lunge for her again. Before I kiss her, I tear at the towel and it drops to the floor. I can't stop myself. I need to have her. Need my hands over her breasts, my lips against the skin of her neck. It seems that all those discussions I had with Rebecca about lacking passion belong to another lifetime. A life before Camille. I dread to think what might have happened if Rebecca had remained in charge of the rental, if she hadn't thrust it upon me like a toy she no longer cared for—kind of like she treated me. If *she* had met Camille. I push the thought away, never wanting to entertain it ever again. Fuck Rebecca. Or no, actually, if she hadn't left me, I wouldn't be standing here being overcome by all of this either.

"We should talk," Camille says.

I drag my lips away from her neck for a second, only to see her head is thrown back all the way—like she's offering herself to me.

"We will," I mumble, my mouth lost somewhere in her hair. I push her down onto the crumpled towel, which can't be very comfortable, but comfort is the last thing on my mind. I kneel in front of her, pull her close, and let my lips roam freely—widely—over her skin. I inhale her, taste her, sink my teeth into her where I can.

I push her down more, until she's leaning back onto her elbows. Her knees are chastely shut in front of me and I push them apart, starting gently but soon overwhelmed by animalistic desire to just have her. Own her. Feel her near as much as I can as long as I still can. I look down at her. The light outside is already fading but I see all I need to see. Camille Rousseau spread out before me. Her eyes eager, pleading. She's been waiting all day as well.

I bow down to kiss her inner thigh, but I'm drawn too much to her sex to spend much time away from it. I want it all. All of her. There's still so much to take, so much to do, so much to find out. As I lean in closer and smell her desire for me, I think about recording this version of myself. About seeing myself in this very moment, ready to devour this woman I... what? Am falling so ridiculously, deliciously, painfully in love with. In that moment, where, granted, I don't have use of all my faculties, I know I will do it. Because there's nothing I wouldn't do for her. I'll travel to Paris. Take the long journey every few months. Stay up late into the night to Skype with her. It all doesn't matter. All that matters is this. My tongue landing on her wet pussy lips. Her taste already so familiar, like I've tasted nothing else over the course of my life. I drag my tongue along her lips. This is no time to be gentle. I barely made it into the door. We're on the kitchen floor. Right underneath the smoke detector.

I lick along her clit, suck it into my mouth greedily. I want this to last but I also want her to come. I want everything. All these impossible things I can't possibly have. Be in the moment, I remind myself. This is now. Later comes later. I dig my hands underneath her bottom and push my fingers into her soft flesh. I lock my mouth onto her clit and just let go. I give her all the power my tongue has, unleashed in a frenzy of licks. If I were to see this woman on a video, I wouldn't recognize her. Of that I'm convinced. Because this doesn't feel like me. With Camille, I feel too alive, too beautiful, too passionate to be the woman whom Rebecca left. Too much the opposite of all the reasons she said she was leaving me for.

"*Mon dieu.*" Camille's fingertips dig into my scalp in return. The more I dig into her, the more she digs into me. We are both lost in this together. Because she might be at the receiving end of my tongue, but I'm just as gone as she is. I'm floating somewhere above, looking down, not believing what I'm seeing. Maybe I need a video for that purpose alone. To merely prove to myself that this is happening, it's possible. It's not some fever dream. We are two real women of flesh and blood, with their hearts on their sleeves. Reduced to nothing but emotion, lust, this *incontournable* desire for each other. For us, there is no other way but this.

"Oh, Zoya." When Camille pronounces my name, she puts the emphasis on the last part. Nobody says it like she does. "Oh," she moans.

She doesn't ask me for anything else, for anything more. No fingers. No directions. As though the desire in my heart has a direct line to hers. We're connected. And I know all of this sounds ludicrous. Like teenagers under the influence of their cruel hormones. Yet, this is how it is. And as Camille shudders beneath me, her body giving itself up to me, her sex pushing into me, I know that Jason was right. I'm in love with her.

CHAPTER TEN

The next day, when Camille and I are on the way to the restaurant to meet Caitlin and Josephine for dinner, Camille asks me all kinds of questions about them, while all I do is regret agreeing to this, because it might only be dinner, and yes, we have to eat, but it cuts brusquely into my time alone with her.

"So, Caitlin is a writer and she works for television as well, and she used to be a professor in the United States," Camille summarizes what I've just told her.

When Caitlin and I set up this dinner on Monday morning—not even forty-eight hours ago—I had no idea that my feelings would intensify even more. That every minute spent away from Camille would feel like trying to write something without the use of my fingers. Not just an inconvenience but like vital parts of me were missing.

"Seeing as you love to google so much, you should google Caitlin some time. She's quite a big deal in the US. Although us Aussies quite like her as well."

"I'll friend her on Facebook. Then I will know all about her," Camille jokes.

Last night, after we couldn't touch anymore of each other because we were raw from too much, I gave her my thoughts on Facebook and social media in general, and how I abhor that the TV network I work for insists we send out a certain number of tweets every week. I never make my quota. When my contract is up for renegotiation, I will have a clause added that stipulates nobody can make me use any social media.

I bump my shoulder into her, relishing in the simple act of walking to a restaurant with her. A simple life with a woman I love. It's all I want. All I need, I think. But life is not simple. And I should really stop using the L word. It makes me feel like I belong to the same demographic as Micky's children.

"When are you going to accept my friend request?" Camille is not done making fun of my, what she called archaic and rigid, stance on Facebook. "I promise I won't invade your privacy any more than I already have."

"I told you. Next time I go on it. On Friday afternoon just before I leave the office."

Camille chuckles, then asks, "Tell me about Josephine."

"Ah, Josephine... Well, you know she works at the Pink Bean part-time. She's also a PhD student. She and Caitlin are co-writing a book. And, perhaps most impressive of all, she's the most wonderful singer." When I think of Josephine singing, I can't help but smile. "I remember the first time we all had dinner together. The entire group. Josephine was so shy. She clearly had the biggest crush on Caitlin. It took her a bit of time to get over the fact that her crush was mutual. It's quite a story."

"And they're in a non-monogamous relationship?"

I shake my head. "I don't think so. Not last I heard, anyway."

"But you said that Caitlin knew all about non-monogamy."

"Oh, she does. Caitlin knows a lot about a great many things." I pull Camille closer to me, wanting everyone we pass to see we are together. "They've only been seeing each other a few months. From what I understand, the beginning of a relationship is usually quite monogamous. But really, if you ask Caitlin, she will tell you all about it. She has made a career of talking about things like this."

Camille leans into me. "I've met them both. There's a bit of an age difference, isn't there?"

"Oh yes. Josephine is only twenty-eight."

"That's barely older than Flo."

"Yes, well, love knows no boundaries or rules or age, I guess."

"Or borders, or distance," Camille adds wistfully.

"I guess we'll have to see about that." We've arrived at the restaurant so there's no time to get into the subject we've been avoiding like the plague. What's going to happen next? We've made our feelings clear to each other in more ways than one, but concrete talk about the future is, for now, still a bridge too far.

Camille gives my hand a good squeeze before we enter. Caitlin and Josephine are already seated. Maybe Camille and I walked slower without knowing, hoping it would slow time as well.

Greetings and kisses are exchanged and then we sit across from each other. Camille sits opposite Caitlin. I'll want to hear every word they exchange. Even though I feel like time is slipping away too quickly, I'm also glad to have this meal with my friends. That way Camille doesn't only exist for me. She will also make an impression on Caitlin and Jo and we can remember this evening together later, when she's gone. It's also nice for Camille to be a part of this aspect of my life. To be embedded in ordinary conversations I have with my friends.

"Okay, first things first," Caitlin says. "I have to tell you something." She looks at me. "When you first hear it, you're not going to like it. That's a given. But I think you might be grateful to me once it sinks in."

I arch up my eyebrows. "What is it?"

"I went behind your back at work. I talked to Jack, found out who this week's guest was on your show. Was relieved to learn it was Harriet Wilton because she and I were on this panel together not long ago. Long story short, I asked her if, as a personal favor to me, she would be willing to postpone the recording of her interview until Friday. She said yes. It's all arranged. You can take Thursday morning off. I know you're going to despise me for this for all of five minutes, after which you will want to hug me for five days. Only you won't be able to because you will be otherwise engaged."

My mouth droops open of its own accord. "You did what?"

Caitlin turns to Josephine. "I told you so."

"Caitlin, this is my work. You can't just mess with that. You can't just talk to Jack, let alone Harriet Wilton and arrange all of this behind my back. That is just completely…" I'm more stupefied than angry.

"The only reason I did it is because I knew you would never do it yourself and you would surely regret it," Caitlin says. "Some things are more important than work. They just are, Zo." She locks her eyes on mine. "And yes, I know I had no right. But I did it anyway. I did it for you, because you are my friend."

"Am I understanding this correctly?" Camille asks. "You will have Thursday morning off?" Her smile is so wide but at the same time, if the dim lights of the restaurant are not playing tricks on me, I can spot the onset of tears in her eyes.

"Looks like it." I can't say anything else. I can't tell Caitlin off when Camille looks at me like this as a result of her actions. I'll hash it out with her later.

"What did you tell Jack?"

"I just told him I needed you for something very personal on Thursday morning, which isn't even a lie."

I shake my head. "I still can't believe you would go behind my back like that." I look at Josephine to gauge what she thinks of all of this, but she just sits there smiling as broadly as Caitlin. They must have concocted this together.

"Thank you very much," Camille says. "I would have

been happy with even an hour extra."

Caitlin tips her head, like a magician who has just performed a successful trick. I guess she has. She doesn't even have me up in arms about it, because, I too, would have been happy with only an hour extra with Camille. Now I'll have an entire morning. We can wake up together. Have breakfast. I can take her to the airport. Wave her off. God, no, I don't want to think about that part just yet. I refocus my attention on the three women I'm having dinner with tonight. Time may be running out, but it doesn't mean I can't make the most of it.

———

"I can't believe you never had a civilized conversation with him," Caitlin says. Wine has flowed freely and we've just all ordered a pousse-café, which Camille has taught us to pronounce without any residue of our native accents. It still doesn't sound as convincing as when she says it. "It could have saved you so much hassle."

"I don't think you quite understand the situation I was in." Camille has given Caitlin and Josephine the short version of her life story—the one I already know by heart. "Yes, at first, it hurt, because I felt like Jean-Claude had broken all our wedding vows in one fell swoop. Until I realized he hadn't. And the one he did break wasn't worth that much to me anyway. Because if not in deed, I had been breaking it in thought for much longer."

Caitlin purses her lips together. "I'm not judging you, Camille. I know things were different back then. And everyone has their own story. I'm just saying that a little honesty can go a long way."

"Let's change the subject," Camille says. "I've talked about my ex-husband enough for one lifetime. Give me some juicy gossip on Zoya instead." She turns to me and winks.

"Zoya is a saint," Caitlin says. "Truly a woman too kind-hearted for her own good."

"Oh, please." I roll my eyes.

The waiter arrives with our drinks. Grand Marnier for Camille and Josephine. Whiskey for Caitlin and me. I'm glad for the interruption. Perhaps bolstered by the favor she has done me by getting me some time off work on Thursday, Caitlin is in a combative mood tonight. Surely what she just said will be followed up by an actual piece of juicy gossip on me.

"Santé!" Camille raises her glass. "It's a pleasure getting to know you all." She swivels in her seat to face me again. "Especially this kind-hearted saint." She leans forward and kisses me on the lips. There's a hint of sadness in the way her lips are folded when her head retreats. I feel it too. I know from experience that great, sweeping emotions like these are often the precursor of an equally great loss.

"The honor has been all ours," Josephine says. "We've all reduced our six degrees of separation to President Dominique Laroche to just the one."

I'm glad I'm not the only Laroche fan girl.

"She is a true modern-day feminist icon," Caitlin says. "If we all come to Paris one day, can you hook us up?"

My mind gets too caught up in the thought of actually going to Paris to see Camille to focus much on the Laroche part. If I were to go, I wouldn't give up a second of my time to spend it with even the most feminist president in the world.

"I can't make any promises, but I could try." Camille is such a tease.

"That's settled then. We're booking our flights tomorrow," Caitlin says. "Zoya must have been creaming her panties ever since you told her about your connection."

I expel a mock sigh and send her a shut-up-already look.

"I think it might be just as interesting to sit down and have a chat with her partner," Josephine says.

Caitlin glances at her and smiles. "The younger partner of a powerful woman. You must be able to identify."

"As far as degrees of power go, honey, you have some

catching up to do." She blows Caitlin a kiss.

"True, but it doesn't stop me from thinking," Caitlin muses. "There must be someone in this country we can back. Some feminist hopeful who will finally, just for starters, have the balls to make same-sex marriage happen. And that's just the tip of the iceberg."

"Politics is at least half ego," Camille says. "You need it to stand for office, to take a swing at grabbing that kind of power. I know many politicians and I can count the truly humble ones on the fingers of half a hand. Even Dominique is not exempt from that."

"There's nothing wrong with a little bit of ego," I say. "As long as you don't surround yourself with yay-sayers and you don't crave perpetual boosting of it."

"That's why Zoya and I are such good friends. When she needs taking down a peg, she calls me." Caitlin raises her almost-empty glass in my direction. "I always take care of her."

Camille turns to me. "For a celebrity, you have very few airs and graces."

"My show doesn't exactly draw huge ratings. I'm mostly well-known among a crowd who wouldn't be caught dead taking a selfie or asking for an autograph."

"Hey," Josephine says, "there's absolutely nothing wrong with respectfully asking for someone's autograph."

"Regardless of that." Camille doesn't know all the details of Caitlin and Josephine's story and keeps her focus on me. "You appear on television on a weekly basis. For quite a few people that's enough of an excuse to behave obnoxiously."

"You've only known her a few days," Caitlin butts in. "She can be quite the princess sometimes." She follows up with a laugh. I hope Camille gets the joke.

Camille responds by throwing an arm around my shoulder. "My beautiful princess. At least for a day and a half longer." She kisses me on the cheek and it shoots straight through me, warming my flesh, quickening my pulse. Counting eight hours at work tomorrow and a few hours of sleep, we have about twenty-four waking hours left together. I think it's time to go.

CHAPTER ELEVEN

After work on Wednesday I rush home. Camille is coming to my house for her last night and morning. We have a lot of plans, and most of them are best executed in my house.

My day has been so hectic—the production schedule is already demanding, and I also had to make up for the time I'll lose tomorrow morning. I haven't had ten spare minutes to myself to come up with the questions I want to ask Camille in our interview. I'm going to have to improvise. Or maybe we can skip directly to the raunchier part of tonight's recording. Because I have said yes. This morning, before work, I told her I would do it. I would make both videos. In the face of all this passion, no matter how foolish and bound by time, trust is not an issue. Besides, we'll both be on the tape. We both have equal amounts of dignity to lose if it ever comes out. And I want that kind of memory of her. No matter how idiotic it sounded when she first brought it up, now I can't imagine the prospect of not having this sensual experience to remember her—us—by. My emotions are too strong for that.

Camille arrives a mere five minutes after I've parked my car. She kisses me deeply and pulls me close, then pushes herself away.

"We have to wait," she says. "Save the best for the camera."

"We could flip things around." I tug her toward me again. "Sex first, interview later."

She ponders this for a few seconds. "A naked interview in bed. I quite like the sound of that."

"I'd be too distracted to ask you any interesting questions. Let's stick to the original plan, which is already crazy enough." I let her go—for now.

"You're in charge, Miss TV Journalist." Camille smiles. "Can I wear something of yours for the first part of the evening's entertainment?" She's wearing a rumpled pair of jeans and an equally wrinkly linen shirt—I assume she's running out of clean clothes and hasn't bothered doing laundry this close to her departure—but she still looks scrumptious.

"Why? You look delicious. Bohemian almost-chic suits you. Must be because you're French and you can wear anything you want and still look effortlessly good in it."

"Oh yes, that's definitely a super power all French citizens are born with."

"Feel free to browse my wardrobe, but I'm not sure you'll find anything that fits. We don't exactly have the same body type."

"I'm sure I'll find something." She shoots me another smile and then, as if she has lived in this house for years, she walks into my bedroom, in search of something camera-friendly to clothe herself in.

While I hear her rummaging around in the other room, I set up the necessary equipment for the interview. I'm not an expert, but I know enough to set up a pair of lamps that will enhance our complexions, and the camera, which is just a point-and-shoot with a decent video function, so it can capture us both in the frame. All we need is a touch of make-up, a few rounds of test shooting, and we're a go.

Camille enters the room in a colorful pull-over dress that I inherited from my grandmother. It's canary yellow and bright orange and every shade in between. It washes out her pale skin tone, but I don't mention it. I'll dim the lights a little and apply some more foundation to her face before I hit record.

———

"What was the highlight of your trip to Australia?" I ask, expecting nothing less than a flippant answer about kangaroos and koalas. It has only taken me a few short days to get accustomed to Camille's sense of humor.

But Camille's facial expression is serious. This interview is no joke to her. "When I arrived at your rental apartment and that smoke detector kept beeping. After two months on the road, and a lot of unexpected encounters and adventures, I had learned that the things that appear the most annoying at first, can lead to the most interesting experiences."

"Really?" I would usually never follow up an interviewee's answer like that, but sitting across from Camille, I can't be expected to keep my composure.

"I am a woman who hasn't traveled much. We went on our yearly family holidays. Provence in summer and Courchevel in winter, but apart from a few city trips in Europe, I had barely left the country. Coming to Australia for two entire months is about the biggest step away from normalcy I could take." She looks at me intently. "Truth be told, the first ten days to two weeks were horrible. I was so out of my depth and I only had myself to rely on. The scenery was stunning, the accommodation just fine, and the people so very nice, but I just couldn't find my groove. It was so bad that, on more than one occasion, I looked up how much it would cost me to cancel my upcoming reservations and change my flight back." She brings two fingers to her chest. "This malaise deep in here. A rupture from my routine, from my everyday life, my children, my house. Not to be able to sit in my favorite chair. Not to stop for coffee in my neighborhood *tabac* before going to work. It was the little things as much as the big things. I don't want to compare the proximity to my children to a cup of coffee at Gérard's, but I missed them both in equal measure. Until I realized that to have a successful trip, I should focus on the little things that could make my stay here great, instead of all the overwhelming big things."

I nod to encourage her to just keep talking, while I hang on every word she says.

"Yes," she continues, "the landscapes were breathtaking, but, in the end, they weren't the real reason I came here. It helped that I could think about my life back home with a gorgeous backdrop, no doubt about that, but the hard work would have to take place inside of me." A tap on the chest again. "And then, little by little, day by day, I started smiling again. I became less flighty. I engaged more with the people I met. I found a routine that pleased me even though I was on the road most of the time. I structured my days so I didn't have to worry so much about details, and could experience maximum freedom."

Come to think of it, I didn't need to prepare any questions. Maybe that's why I didn't. Because I subconsciously knew that Camille would just talk—and I would get to know her better and appreciate her even more in the process.

"Traveling alone gives you a lot of time to think. A lot." She inserts a light chuckle. "Too much at times, I guess. Because I do believe there's a danger in overthinking. I've always been more a woman of action. I'm a mother. Action has been my go-to mode for the past twenty-five years." She falls silent for a few seconds.

My turn. "What will be the first thing you do when you get back to Paris?"

She purses her lips together. "I land on Friday morning. Deliberately timed that way because it's a public holiday in France, so I can have breakfast with my children. Ben will be coming up from Marseille for the long weekend. He'll pick me up from the airport and we'll go to Flo's together." Her voice breaks a little. She breathes in deeply, takes a few more seconds, recrosses her legs. "I miss them so much. It has come and gone in waves. In the beginning, it was really bad. I was Skyping them every other day. Then as I got more comfortable, I managed to keep my distance—literally and figuratively. But now, so close to seeing them again, it can sometimes well up in me with such force."

"Not long now." My own voice doesn't sound so stable.

"Then I met you." A feeble smile appears on her face. "And I already know I'm going to miss you like crazy."

Maybe this is when we talk about it, address the elephant that's been in the room with us for a few days now. We'll have it on tape forever if we do.

"Are you sure I can't put you in my suitcase? Sneak you out of the country unnoticed so no one will give you a hard time about it?"

"Getting a half day off work already required Caitlin talking to my producer behind my back. The show's season is long, and there are still quite a few weeks to go."

"When is your last show?" Camille squirms in her seat.

"Early July."

"Come to Paris in July, then. Fifty percent of the locals leave town after the *quatorze*. It'll be like having the city all to ourselves."

"You want me to come to Paris?"

Her nod starts small at first, but soon transforms into an extremely convincing one. "Of course I do."

"You say that now, but July is still two months away."

"So?" I can tell she's itching to get out of her chair. "Two months is nothing."

"Two months of what?" It's excruciating to be thinking of a camera while having this conversation. But when a camera is trained on me, I'm always aware of it. I can't help it.

She sucks the inside of her cheek into her mouth. It makes a cute smacking sound when she lets it inflate again. "Longing. Pent-up desire. Love notes. I don't really know, Zoya."

"You mean a long-distance relationship?"

"Wouldn't it be the cruelest thing of all not to try?" She scoots up out of her chair, crouches in front of me and takes my hands in hers. "I know I want to. At least try. I can't not."

"I want to as well." A smile of pure joy spreads on my lips. To just say it after barely wanting to think about it for the past few days is liberating.

"Then let's do it. We have the Internet. We can talk as if you're in the next room. And since you're ahead in time, I can find a sickly-sweet email from you in my inbox every morning." Camille's smile equals mine.

"As long as you send me one back every evening…" I chuckle. "I'll have to find a way to miraculously internalize time zones. That always messes with my head."

"There are apps for that. There are apps for everything these days." Camille swallows hard. "Summer in Paris is beautiful. I can't wait to spend it with you."

"Okay." Camille stands and I let her pull me up. "It's a deal."

Before she kisses me, she says, "You didn't think I would get on that plane and disappear from your life forever?"

"I could think it but I couldn't imagine it."

Camille presses herself against me.

"You're not wearing a bra," I murmur. "We might have to redo the interview."

"I'm not wearing any underwear either." She pulls up the dress, takes my hand, and brings it between her legs.

"I guess it's time for part two of the evening."

"Interview me on Skype when I'm back in France. It will give us something to talk about." She pushes my hand so high between her thighs I can feel her wetness. "This is our last night together. Let's make the most of it."

CHAPTER TWELVE

In between gropes and kisses, we've moved the recording equipment to my bedroom. There's no time for a test shoot or to set up special lighting. It might be that only our buttocks or just shadows are visible when we look at the video later. But I don't care. Because this is not a performance. Camille and I have slept together a lot since we first met—I've had numerous orgasms and countless hours of the most exquisite fun—but this time, it's different. It's far removed from the first, more hesitant time. Tonight, in my bed, we're making a promise to each other. And we have no choice but to call this a relationship, albeit long-distance. It's implied in the term. Perhaps, if she lived here, we'd be dating. Or going out. But, in the end, it would all just be a matter of silly semantics. Because I'm in love with her, and she is with me. And we have no way of knowing whether our infatuation will survive the distance between us, and whether it's strong enough to turn into something more. We have no crystal ball. All we have are our feelings.

The yellow dress is already discarded next to the bed, on which Camille lies stark naked. I want to dive in and devour her, and take my time and savor her in equal measure. Maybe I can do both. Devour first, savor later.

I'm still in my work clothes. I look at her, take in her svelte form, while I clumsily step out of my shoes and tug at my clothes, not able to remove them fast enough.

By the time I finally lie down next to her, I feel a little

exhausted just because of all the building anticipation.

"I had so many things left I wanted to ask you," I say.

"Ditto." Camille scoots closer to me. "But talking is something we can do over the phone. This is not." She pulls me close, her kiss deep from the start.

I can't imagine waking up on Friday and having no one to kiss like this. Was it only last Friday that I met her? It seems like a lifetime ago. A lifetime of intimacy and intensity compressed into less than a week. It's madness, but a madness hinged on a truth that can't be denied. Or are my feelings not real? Will they gradually lose steam as the days increase the distance between us? As she picks her life back up in Paris. Slips back into the mundane. Spends time with her family, friends and colleagues. Because I can't imagine my life going back to how it was before I met her. The emotional residue of my break-up with Rebecca. Welcoming new guests to the apartment. I want to take the listing off the website straight away so no one else can sleep there and erase Camille's presence, undo her memory.

"Hey." Her hands are in my hair. Her face is so close. "It's going to be all right." She kisses me on the nose. "If it's meant to be, it's meant to be."

I nod, biting back tears.

She runs a fingertip over my arm, leaving a field of goosebumps in its wake. "You're so beautiful."

"Say it in French," I ask.

"*Tu es si belle.*" Her fingertip glides up again. "*Si ravissante.*"

Before I kiss her again, I vow to myself to learn French. I'll watch French movies, listen to French songs in the car. Anything to make me feel closer to her.

Our bodies are pressed together. The warmth of her skin is soothing and arousing at the same time. I want her, but I want to lie here like this for a long while as well. I want everything I can't have.

"*Je te veux,*" Camille says. And my brain might not know

what it means, but my heart does. Even if she hadn't spoken a word of English, I still would have fallen in love with her. *Incontournable.*

Camille brings a hand to my breast and lightly cups it in her palm. I look down, at her pale skin against my brown one. At how my flesh spills over her fingers. At all the physical differences between us. Emotionally, right now, we are one and the same. We live on the same page. We both want the exact same thing. For this night to never end. And if it does, for this memory to last forever, to feed our souls over distance and time.

Camille's hand becomes more insistent. She slides down a little, brings my breast to her mouth, and takes my nipple between her lips. She uses her teeth and the sudden jolt of pain is so exquisite, a moan escapes my throat. With her, everything feels like it is being done to me thousandfold. The intensity dialed up to maximum strength. It doesn't seem possible to feel any more than I do when I'm with her.

She pushes me onto my back and focuses her attention on my other breast and nipple. She gives them the same treatment: hand squeezing, teeth sinking in.

Camille doesn't say anything in French anymore. We've gone beyond words. The way she looks at me says enough— more than words ever could. Her gaze sweeps over my naked body while her fingers glide along my skin. Is this really a woman who just a week ago had never slept with another female? Did the lust between us elevate her lovemaking skills to expert level? Or, perhaps, it's not about skill and experience at all. It's about emotions. How we are together in these moments. Connected. Our truest selves. Bound by this mysterious spell that was cast upon us when we met.

Her gaze finds mine. She looks at me and her lips draw into a sly smile. "I've been fantasizing about something," she says.

"Have you?"

She just nods, doesn't say anything else for a while, just

looks at me.

Then she speaks again. "It kind of feels like now or... well, not never, but at least not for a good long while."

A smile breaks out on my face. I grab her by the wrist and bring her hand to my mouth. "Tell me."

"Can I show you instead?"

I nod and wait. Every cell in my body is filled with anticipation. Will she ask me to turn around and spank my ass? Ask me to spank hers? Does she want me to tie her up? I may have a decade-old pair of handcuffs in a drawer somewhere.

Camille keeps her eyes on me, pushes herself onto her knees, then swings one leg over my body to straddle me. She pauses, scans my face again.

I nod to encourage her. This could still go in many directions, although I gather no spanking will be involved.

My eyes are drawn to her spread legs. How I want to feast on her there, extract every last drop from her. Her knees start shuffling toward my face. Oh. I think I know where this is going.

"Tell me if you don't like it," she says, a little tremor in her voice. The shakiness of her tone surprises me, because, from the very beginning Camille has been so assured in the bedroom.

"I promise." I can't keep a grin off my face. "But I think I'll like it."

She smiles back, her confidence has returned. The tripod with camera stands on the side of the bed, and she turns her head and looks into the lens. I can't wait to see the footage. I can relive this moment many times over. I can see her look at me the way she just did again and again.

Camille scoots closer to my face. Then she's so close I can smell her most intimate perfume. A few more wriggles of her body and her sex hovers over my mouth. Before she brings it within reach of my lips and tongue, she looks down at me. Her eyes are different. More alive with a mischievous sparkle. The eyes of someone whose fantasy is about to become reality.

She hunkers down and I clasp my hands against her ass cheeks. Pull her to me. Even though the action is localized to my mouth and her pussy, it feels like she's all over me. I can sense her everywhere. I close my eyes because I can't see much, and everything intensifies even more.

I slide the tip of my tongue over her pussy lips, let it skate over her clit. Camille squirms on top of me. She's not only realizing a fantasy, but she'll also have it on video. Well played on her part.

I repeat the motion of my tongue a few times, tasting her almost tentatively. This evening is not a race to the finish. It's not about climax after climax. It's about committing to memory. How she smells, feels, tastes. The sounds she makes in the back of her throat when she's about to come. The sensation of her flesh in my eager hands.

I circle her clit with my tongue, suck it into my mouth, then trill the tip of my tongue over it for a few seconds. She trembles in my hands. The sound of her voice is muffled by her knees next to my ears. I can't wait to watch this on video either. To see her when she gives herself up like this. It will be a deliciously kinky privilege.

I up the ante of my tongue action. I suck at her clit as though I want to suck her entire being inside of me. As though it will allow me to keep a part of her within me, resting there, until it can be replenished when I see her again.

Then I feel her hand on mine, which still resides on her ass. She takes control of it and guides it closer to the split between her cheeks. She doesn't let go until the tip of my middle finger rests next to the rim of her most intimate orifice. I guess her fantasy was more elaborate than just sitting on my face. She gives my hand a squeeze. It's the only way we have of communicating while my mouth is busy and my ears are deaf. But I know what to do. I want to give Camille everything she wants that is within my capabilities.

This certainly is.

I move my finger down a little and coat it in her abundant wetness. Then I bring it back and I slide in the tip. I focus on my hand for a few seconds, my tongue going limp against her clit. My fingertip is met with such fierce warmth, it spurs my tongue back into action.

"Oh." Camille's groan is so wild I can hear it loud and clear. She wiggles her ass a bit, inches it closer to my finger. She wants more. I slide in a little deeper while my tongue goes crazy against her clit. The contrast between the gentle movements of my finger and the frenzy of my tongue is startling. It makes my own blood beat faster in my veins. But nothing is more important to me right now than giving Camille the orgasm she's been dreaming of—perhaps for years.

Her voice increases in pitch. She moans loudly, as though the sound comes from the deepest place within her. She shivers against my finger. Her movements grow more out of control. She bucks against my mouth, against my finger, sucking it deeper inside of herself. Then she goes totally still for a few seconds, during which I don't dare move.

Her yelp is so heartfelt, it has me worried for an instant. But then she maneuvers herself away from my finger and mouth, and pushes herself off me. She doesn't smile when she looks down at me. She just crashes next to me and looks me in the eyes, then kisses me full on the lips.

———

After I've washed my hands and am lying next to Camille in my bed again—where I want to preserve the imprint she is making in my mattress forever—she sends me a big smile, and says, "I would like to amend my answer to one of your questions from earlier. Namely the highlight of my trip to Australia." She leans her head on an upturned palm. "I've had many highlights, but nothing beats the feeling of making another woman climax." Her smile goes soft. "There's truly nothing like it."

"Agreed."

She arches up her eyebrows. "I feel like I have so many climaxes to make up for. Mine and others…" She paints a circle around my belly-button. My body responds accordingly. "And by others, I mean you."

Though my body is in a high state of arousal, there's one thing we haven't yet addressed. "I wouldn't want to limit your new-found sources of pleasure when you are back in Paris."

"What do you mean?"

"I mean that we're not going to see each other for at least two months. You've just learned all about the gratification of being with another woman. We can talk about this. If you want to… explore."

"I've waited a long time for this. I'm sure I can wait a little longer for more."

"I would understand, is all I'm saying."

"Will you be exploring your *pleasure* with other women?" she asks, her finger still circling my navel.

"God no." I smile up at her. "I'm pretty convinced no other woman can make me feel like this."

"Like what?" Camille smiles at me coyly as she lets her finger dip lower. "Can you describe it for me?" Her voice has gone low.

"How about I show you instead?" I repeat her words from earlier.

"That works for me." Her finger has drifted all the way between my legs.

Instinctively, I spread them more. It's only the tip of her finger touching me, yet it feels like so much more. My body responds as though Camille has her hands all over me. My back arches up to her. My whole being is attuned to her. The first time we ended up in bed together, it still felt like I was trying to exorcise the last remnants of Rebecca's presence from my mind. Now, it's all about Camille. Everything associated with Rebecca feels like a lifetime ago. My life before Camille. The life that will, in a way, end tomorrow already. Better make the most of it now. No more thoughts about our upcoming farewell. I need to believe that there's only now.

It's not difficult, because Camille's finger is skating along my throbbing pussy lips. She kisses me, then slides her body down. As she does, I find the camera and glance into the lens. I want to know what I look like in this moment. I want to remember it forever. These delicious few seconds of extreme anticipation. Her finger hovers, but it's near enough. She sits between my legs and looks at me. To have this woman look at me like that. She looks like she's about to lick her lips, but there's awe in her face as well. I wish I had set up a camera at the head of the bed so her expression right now could have been captured as well.

She bows down. Both her hands are on my hips. She digs her nails into my soft flesh there. Then she folds her long body in half and touches her tongue to my lips. Slowly, she drags the tip up and down. It shoots through me like a dagger of red, hot lust. Tears prick behind my eyes. It's the combination of her and me. It's as if my subconscious realizes there's some sort of magic in it. And all the chemical processes in my brain and body are working together to make me even more crazy about Camille Rousseau. Even her name sounds so delicious. My girlfriend, Camille Rousseau. It sounds so sophisticated. In my head, it sounds so real.

Her tongue is drawing circles now, and I don't even need her to add any fingers. I can still taste her on my own tongue. I can still feel her heat on the tip of my finger. My arousal has grown to such levels, it doesn't even matter what she does anymore. Because that's Camille Rousseau's tongue on my clit. Camille Rousseau with her small dark eyes. Her freckled, pale skin. Her long, gangly limbs. Her French sense of humor. The person is enough. The sight of her bowed down in front of me catapults me easily onto the next plane of arousal. But most of all, this is us. Camille and Zoya. In this bed on this night. I look into the lens again. That way I'll be able to examine the changes in my face as Camille brings me closer to orgasm. I'm not far off now.

I feel a finger at the entrance of my pussy. Two. She spreads my lips. There's a shift of air. She's no longer licking me. She's looking. Involuntarily, I buck up my hips.

Two fingers pierce me. Or is it three? I have no idea, but she spreads me wide. My pussy clamps down on her, wanting to trap her there forever.

Camille fucks me slowly and I feel it everywhere. Not only in my flesh, that sparks with heat and lust and anticipatory satisfaction, but it echoes throughout me so that my mind is filled with only her. Camille Rousseau. I forget about everything else—myself most of all. It's all her—and me tethered to her fingers inside of me. And, oh, they feel so good. Camille has the kind of fingers I can just look at and get aroused. They're slender, like her, and long and strong. I bet that, to most, she has the most ordinary hands, but to me, like her, they're special. Especially because of what they're doing right now. Burrowing into me, igniting my pleasure, calling it. But I don't want to come just yet. I want this exquisite sensation of almost-but-not-yet to last a little longer. Want her fingers to remain for as long as I can take them.

I open my eyes and find her looking at me. I stare back and her gaze on me unleashes something. Tears first of all. The tears that have been welling behind my eyes break free. Because she is releasing more in me than orgasmic endorphins and this powerful blend of love and lust. Before I met her, I was bitter and angry. I felt slighted and wronged by the woman I loved. I felt sorry for myself and allowed myself to wallow in it endlessly. Camille put a stop to all of that when she asked me out.

I look into her eyes as tears stream down my cheeks. *Wetness all around*, I think, as her fingers keep delving down, keep taking me. She brings her other hand to my belly, then lower, and lower still. She flicks a finger over my clit while she keeps looking at me. I know what she's doing. She wants the memory of my face, wants to remember what I look like when I come for her.

I want to keep my eyes open. I want that connection between us when I tip over the edge. That little something extra to make it more intimate.

She circles my clit with her fingertip while the fingers of her other hand become more insistent inside of me. Her strokes pick up speed, find a rhythm with the action she bestows on my clit. Her eyes are narrowed. The room is semi-dark, but I can still make out the freckles on her nose. The curve of her delicious lips, which are parted now—as though she's right along on the path to ecstasy with me.

"Oh god," I moan. "Oh, Camille." Saying her name is the very thing that pushes me over. And as the heat engulfs me, and the white light erupts inside my mind, for the life of me, I can't keep my eyes open. But even when my eyelids fall shut, she is still all I see. There's no one or nothing else.

When I come to and open my eyes, a soft smile plays on her lips. Her fingers retreat and, in a gesture that has already become quite predictable, she brings them to her mouth and licks them. It's enough for me to want them buried deep inside of me again. To want to repeat this all night long. I really do owe Caitlin for getting me the morning off tomorrow. Right now, it's everything. Nothing is more important. Because it's not just the extra few hours tomorrow, but the effect they have on tonight. It adds a carefreeness we need right now.

"You showed me," she says. "I've seen more than enough." She flanks my body with hers and kisses me. "I think we should reposition the camera now."

CHAPTER THIRTEEN

The morning comes too soon, even though we have done everything possible to make time slow down. Nothing worked. Time just kept marching on, which, we concluded, would help us during the two months we'll spend apart.

"No tears," Camille says just after we've woken up. "What happened to us is a good thing. A glorious thing. Tears will only ruin it."

"I'll try." I remember my tears from last night vividly, how they ran hotly over my cheeks, then pooled into a cold mess on my neck. "I promise."

"I'll call you when I get to Hong Kong. It'll be evening here."

"My phone won't leave my side all day."

"I will write you a long email when I'm on the plane."

"God, it's such a long journey."

"Nine hours to Hong Kong. Five hour lay-over. Then thirteen hours to Paris. It's not for the faint of heart." She chuckles.

"My heart won't be faint when I embark on the same journey in two months. I'll book my ticket today."

"Hopefully you'll still want to come by then."

"I can't think of any reason why not."

"Hm." Camille pretends to be thinking deeply. "What if… Dominique Laroche invites me for a threesome with her and Stéphanie?"

"Then you'd better tell her to wait until July so we can

make it a foursome."

"I think we might be too old for her anyway." She's giggling like a schoolgirl. She scoots closer to me, if that's even possible, her leg over mine, her warm body pressed to me, her arm wound tightly around my torso. "I don't want to go home."

"Your children are waiting for you at the other end of that journey," I say, instead of what I really want to say. That I don't want her to go either. But I promised her no tears and if we start talking like that there will be no holding back.

"I have to go back to work," she groans.

"I'm sure French science has missed you," I say into her hair.

"I'm not so sure I missed it."

"The routine will help."

"My poor neglected cat will be happy to be able to return home. She's been staying with my neighbor."

"You have a cat?" That's the first time I've heard Camille mention any pets.

"Yes. Her name is Iris. She's huge and black as coal and I'm sure she missed her territory more than her human."

"Do you have any other pets?"

Camille shakes her head against my shoulder. "No. It's just me and Iris."

"After Rebecca left, I thought about getting a cat. But then I thought it better to move house first."

"That's a good idea." She pulls her face away from my shoulder and looks at me. "Are you going to move into the Airbnb now?"

"That bloody apartment. I never wanted it. The whole Airbnb enterprise was Rebecca's baby. I went to see the place with her before she bought it, and I had to sign the papers because it was bought in my name, but that's about it. And look what it ended up doing to me."

"If the place was her baby, how come you ended up in charge?"

"Let's just say her interests changed." I kiss Camille on the cheek. "But let's not waste our time talking about my ex."

Camille nods and silence falls. "Would it be easier for you if you didn't come to the airport?" she asks.

"Maybe, but even if it was, I would still go. Unless you don't want me to."

"I want you to get on that plane with me. That's what I want."

"For what it's worth, if it wasn't for my job, I'd fly to Paris with you in a heartbeat. It would be different if you lived in Brussels or another boring sounding city like that, but Paris... oh, yes."

"So, it would be more the city than the woman?" She grins. "I get it."

"The no-tears thing we were talking about. Does it also count in the shower where you can't see them?" I dig my fingertips into her biceps. "Because I'm about ready for a wash now."

Because I don't trust myself to drive back safely after saying goodbye to Camille, we take a taxi to the airport. It's a beautiful day and we spend most of the way there gazing out of the window, fighting with our emotions—trying not to cry.

I'm wearing sunglasses and a hat, because at the airport just when I'm saying goodbye to a woman I've fallen in love with over the course of one short week, is not a time I want to be recognized by anyone. I wouldn't usually bother, but today, I've made the effort.

When we arrive, she checks in first so she can be rid of her luggage—which is surprisingly light for a two-month trip —and then the time has come. We're in a public space, so a drawn-out kissing session is out of the question. I can't go past security with her. All we can do now is have coffee together.

"They should have special cubicles or something where

people can say goodbye to each other properly without needing to resort to awkward public displays of affection," I say, when I sit across from Camille for the last time. I gave her the yellow dress she wore last night, and, on her insistence, a scarf of mine with my perfume on. But for the long-haul flight she's wearing comfortable jeans, T-shirt and a blazer.

"Imagine what people would do in those things, though," Camille says. "A few last minutes of passion before boarding." She shakes her head. "Permanent cleaning staff would be required."

"Yeah." I've scooted my chair close to hers so I can at least put a hand on her knee.

"I'm going to have to go soon." She checks her watch. "We stayed in the shower too long." She puts her head on my shoulder. "It was worth every minute."

"Call me as soon as you can." I'm beginning to sound like a broken record.

She nods. "It's been a while since I had someone waiting by the phone for me to call."

"Are you going to tell your children?"

"I can't see how I can keep it a secret from them. They'll probably be able to read it off my face as soon as they see me." She drains the last of her coffee, starts pushing her chair back.

The dreaded moment has come. Maybe it won't be so bad. Maybe the hours leading up to it will have taken out most of the sting.

"I'll walk with you." I take her hand in mine. The line at security is long, but I can't line up with her. I can wait until she has disappeared behind the panels dividing the departure hall from the inner sanctum of the airport. I'll see her inch closer to the spot where she will disappear from my sight. Then I'll take a taxi straight to work.

"Bye, my love." She turns to me, puts her cool hands on my neck. "I'm going to miss you so much, but I'm trying to look at it from the bright side. It was a privilege getting to know you, Zoya Das. And I'll have hours of your show to watch on the flight."

"I'll edit our videos, then find some way to encrypt them before sending them to you."

"See, we both have enticing prospects."

"Two months is nothing." I kiss her on the lips, let my tongue slide in because time is running out now, and it's the closest I can still get.

"Bye," she says again. "We'll talk in about ten hours."

"I'll try to stay awake after you kept me up most of the night."

"I'm so not sorry about that." She looks me in the eyes. "I'm going now."

But she doesn't go. She stands there with me for a few more seconds as I feel my heart sink and my stomach clench into a coil I never expect to recover from. I'll have to stop eating until I see her again. Until I can feast on the delicious foods of Paris. I'll be as slender as her. My mind doesn't know what to think. I don't know what to do. I don't want to let go of her hand, but I don't want to make a scene at the airport. I want her very last memory of me to be a good one.

"*Au revoir*," she says, kisses me lightly on the lips, lets her hand slide out of mine and turns around. The queue has become a little shorter, but she'll still have to wait. I can still look at her for a while.

I study her posture. Camille is not looking at me; she's staring ahead, straight-backed. The sight of her profile alone is enough to drive me mad with longing already. In the grand scheme of things, two months might be nothing, but it feels like about a decade to me now.

Have some perspective, Zoya, I think. *Keep looking on the bright side.* After all, this might not have happened at all. If Myrtle hadn't been sick. If I'd asked Caitlin to deliver a pack of batteries to the Airbnb because it's only a five minute walk from her place. If I had said no when Camille asked me out because of that disastrous afternoon with Rebecca.

Camille's advancing in the line too quickly. She turns her head. Her gaze finds mine. She sends me a small smile. I wish it was me standing in that line already. Two months from now. Embarking on the long journey to see her.

I might be determined to book my ticket this very day, but, of course, it's not certain that everything will work out. There are so many factors. For her, it could still turn out to be a holiday fling in faraway Australia. Something, she could soon realize, from another time in her life.

I wave at her but there's no conviction in my action. She's only a few yards from me, but she feels so far away already. This is the real torture, watching how she slowly slips out of my life.

I stay rooted to my spot for long minutes after she's passed security and is no longer in my sight. I'm hoping for a miracle. A canceled flight. Anything that will make her walk back through that gate. To make her return to me. To not have her live in Paris. But then she wouldn't be the same woman. Our few days together wouldn't have been so intense.

After ten minutes, I take a deep breath, bite back the tears—because, even though she is gone now, I still want to keep my promise to her—and leave the airport.

CHAPTER FOURTEEN

On Friday night, I don't want to go to the open mic night at the Pink Bean. I want to stay home and wait for Camille to call. I spoke to her last night when she was on her stopover in Hong Kong, but she was in an airport lounge and couldn't exactly whisper sweet nothings in my ear. It was a short, quite matter-of-fact conversation, that left me wanting so much more.

Since then, she has texted me to say she has arrived safely in Paris, but I haven't received that email she joked about before she left. There's an eight-hour time difference between Sydney and Paris. After work for me would be a perfect time to Skype.

Goodness, I feel like a teenager tracking her first girlfriend's every move. Wanting to know every little thing she does. Just to feel a connection, and not merely this sense of loss that keeps expanding in my chest.

I text Caitlin to let her know I'll come to hear Josephine sing next time. I know that if I call her, she'll try to talk me out of it with a slew of rational arguments I might even want to cling to, just to stop myself from feeling like this. But, truth be told, this lovesickness—I don't know how else to describe it—is something I cherish as well. Because, as it turns out, after the whole Rebecca debacle, I *can* still fall in love. Her cheating on me hasn't ruined me for the rest of my life. Going on a date with Camille was only meant to be a distraction with a woman who was meant to be unavailable, but it has turned into so much more. Although the unavailable part still holds true.

I'll stay home and look at the videos I've been afraid to download to my laptop. I'm afraid of the emotions they'll provoke and my incapacity to handle them.

I've barely sent my text, when Caitlin calls. I should have known. Perhaps I did.

"I'm not having you sit in your house by yourself all night pining for Camille. There's just no way, Zo," she says, dispensing with the greetings. "Come out with us. And that's an order."

"Last time I checked Jack was my boss, not you," I reply.

"I'll send a car to your house and have the driver honk the horn until you get in. Your neighbors will hate you for disturbing their Friday night Balmain peace."

I sigh. "I just don't feel like company that much."

"Of course you don't, but that's not the point." Caitlin's voice softens a little. "When we all went to dinner that night, and you went to the ladies', I promised Camille I would not let this happen. I promised I would do everything I could to get you out of the house, where all you will do is mope and wait for the phone to ring. Do you really want me to break a promise to Camille?"

"Remind me to never get on your bad side." I chuckle. "You're like a starving pit-bull with a bone."

"I'm your friend. I'm looking out for you. Come spend some time with us. Stay over at mine. We'll have a big breakfast at the Pink Bean tomorrow morning. It will be fun."

"But... what if she calls?" As soon as the words leave my mouth I know how they make me sound.

"Then you pick up the damn phone. You don't have to be in your house to talk to her. Two decades ago, there was this invention called a mobile phone. I'm sure you can use Sheryl and Kristin's apartment if you want some privacy.

Besides, she wouldn't just call. She would let you know first. Camille has been on a long journey and is probably suffering from jet lag right now. Give her some time to recover. And come out with us. I can probably sneak in some booze if it would make you feel any better."

"Fine."

"To the booze or to coming out?" Caitlin asks.

"Both," I say.

———

The open mic is a Josephine Greenwood special, for which everyone has turned up, it seems. Or perhaps Caitlin has drummed up all the others for moral support in dealing with me. Micky gives me the kind of hug I've never received from her before and Amber looks at me with something that feels like pity in her glance.

"I thought the idea was to cheer me up," I whisper to Caitlin. "What's with the funeral vibe?"

"They don't know how to behave around you," she says. "I'll sort them out."

Caitlin James. My savior. It's as though she's turned into the big sister who always has my back.

Josephine is getting ready on the stage. Kristin introduces her, although no one present here still needs to be introduced to Josephine Greenwood. Every single person has come to hear her sing. Now that they still can in this intimate setting. Kristin has to hire an extra barista for these monthly events, which keep increasing in audience size as word has spread about Josephine's voice.

I can still remember the first time I heard her sing, when she flabbergasted us all with the intensity and sheer beauty of her voice. In that sense, it's not a chore to come here. By the time I take my seat, I'm glad Caitlin convinced me. Being near my friends is better than staying at home and waiting for news from Camille. I'm a grown woman. I shouldn't be waiting by the phone like that. Perhaps I shouldn't have gone and fallen in love with a French woman passing through either, but there you have it.

Josephine has grown much more confident on the stage and she has a real charming presence up there now, cracking jokes in between songs—and not sparing Caitlin when she does, which makes her a girl after my own heart. Caitlin always sits beaming with pride whenever Josephine takes to the stage, as though she turns into a different person when her girlfriend is singing. Caitlin is not really the adoring girlfriend type who pines for her lover when she's not there —the opposite of the way I feel right now—except when Josephine sings. Then her eyes soften, her whole being relaxes, and she listens with rapture in her glance. Josephine might have started out as a Caitlin James fangirl but, from where I'm sitting, it looks like the tables have turned.

At times, it was hard to witness her falling in love after my break-up with Rebecca. Selfish as it may sound, when your heart has just been broken into a million pieces, being faced with young love like that can be quite crushing. Because it made me realize what I was missing. Made me observe closely what love can do to a person. Made me remember what passion looked like. And it made me realize that, perhaps, at times, I couldn't give Rebecca what she so craved anymore.

Josephine starts singing and I keep one hand on my mobile, which I've put in my jeans pocket, in case it vibrates. Of course she sings a love song, which makes me miss Camille even more, but it's also soothing in a way. Two months is nothing, I repeat to myself. I have to, not only because I need it as a mantra, but also because I don't want to think beyond those two months. I've reserved my ticket to Paris already. I still need to confirm it after I have a conversation with my boss and with Camille, but I have it locked down. I can go to Paris for a few weeks. After that, I will have to return to Australia. And then what? That's what I don't want to think about, but my thoughts keep drifting as Josephine sings.

"I would like to dedicate the next song to my friend Zoya," she says. "She'll know why." I perk up at the mention of my name. Josephine shoots me a wink from the stage. "I wrote it myself and it's called 'Faraway Dreams,'" Josephine says.

I clap along with the crowd, hoping I'll be able to keep it dry. As I listen to the words, it's obvious the song is actually about Caitlin, and how faraway she appeared to Josephine for a while, but I guess the lyrics can apply to my situation in a way.

Just as I sit after thanking Jo with a standing ovation, there's a vibration in my pocket. My heart leaps into my throat. With trembling hands, I slide my phone out. A text from Camille. *Bonsoir Sydney*, it says, and it's accompanied by a picture of her blowing me a kiss. *I just sent you that email*, it continues. *I've been working on it since I was waiting for my plane to leave yesterday—or whatever day it was.*

Camille sent me an email. Something unclenches in my stomach. Something I've been holding on to since she left. As though I was waiting for a sign that we were, somehow, still on. That she didn't decide to forget about me as soon as she set foot on French soil. Because it's too hard to be in love with someone living on the other side of the world. Because on her journey to find herself, she did. And she's ready to take up a new life. A better one. I don't know anything about the Parisian lesbian scene, but I can only imagine quite a few women would like to take her out for cheese and wine—and more.

While Josephine launches into the next song, I open my email application and impatiently wait for Camille's email to come in. Then there it is. In black and white on my screen.

Caitlin is too wrapped up in Josephine's performance to pay attention to my phone shenanigans. My pulse picks up speed as I tap to open it.

Mon Amour,

Zoya,

Have I told you how much I like your name? The way it sounds and makes me feel when it rolls off my tongue? I found myself crazily whispering it out loud on the plane. I don't know any other Zoyas. You're the only one.

I didn't actually write this on the plane. But I thought about it. I composed it in my head over and over again to make time go by faster. Even though the faster time went, the farther I was taken away from you. Everything seems to have turned into this double-edged sword now that I've met you.

I have a confession to make. Once I made it past security, I cried. Not a lot. Not enough to embarrass myself—not that I care much about that—but the tears just spilled from my eyes all of a sudden. It was unstoppable. Because you have done something to me. And you're in my heart, but you're so far away. I wonder what you'll be doing when you get this. Have you watched our video yet?

I take a deep breath and avert my gaze from the screen for a few seconds. Her words are creating a tidal wave behind my eyes. I can't stay here; as soon as this song ends, I'll ask Sheryl if I can go upstairs. I look around. I find Robin staring at me. What would she do if work took her back to the States? She wouldn't go. I give her a small smile. She just moved in with Micky. From what Micky has told me, Robin wasn't meant to stay in Sydney long-term, but she changed her plans. For love.

Once upstairs, I read the rest of the email.

I watched as many episodes of your show as I could, until my eyes hurt so much, I couldn't keep them open. But of course, I couldn't sleep. My thoughts were too preoccupied with you. Do I sound like a lovesick teenager? But I miss you so much already. Will you call me when you get this? I don't care what time it is. I'll happily wake up for you. I want to hear your voice, if only to make sure you're real, and not some figment of my imagination. Did I lose my mind back in Australia? If so, whose email address is this? ;-)

I stop reading and scroll to her number. My heart beats in my throat as the phone rings. She picks up after two beeps.

"That was quick," she says, and I can so clearly hear the smile in her voice.

"I'm at your beck and call, no matter the time zone I'm in."

"Hey." Her voice goes soft. "How are you?"

"Good now that I'm talking to you." I take a deep breath. She hasn't forgotten about me just yet. Distance hasn't undone our mad feelings for each other. "Thank you for your email."

"I expect one in return."

We banter for a while and she tells me about her uneventful flight and going to fetch her cat, who hasn't left her side since, and seeing her children again.

"Have you booked that flight as you promised?" she asks then.

"I just need to confirm it, but I wanted to double check with you first."

"There's nothing to double check, Zoya. As soon as you're off work, come see me. Please."

"I will." Inside, I feel warm and fuzzy.

"Good. Can you get Caitlin to call your boss again and pull some strings so your show ends sooner?" She follows up with a chuckle.

"I'm quite sure not even Caitlin has that kind of sway with the network."

"Pity." Her voice is but a whisper. "I had a lot of time to think," she says. "Are we crazy for doing this? For feeling like this?"

"No." My tone is adamant. "Not crazy. We just fell in love."

"Which is, in itself, a sort of temporary insanity," she replies.

"Well, you're the scientist."

"And you're the journalist. Between us, we should be able to figure it out."

"There's not much to figure out. All we need is patience."

"As I said before, it took me until I was forty-nine to find you, and I had to travel many miles for it. I can wait a little longer."

The question I haven't been able to keep from popping up is there at the forefront of my brain again. "What happens after Paris, though?" If I can't ask Camille, who can I ask?

"I don't know, *mon amour*. The next step, whatever that may be at the time."

"You're right. We shouldn't get ahead of ourselves."

"Instead of asking impossible questions, here are a few things you can do to keep yourself occupied. Do you have a pen to write this down?" The smile in her voice is back. "One: reply to my email. Two: send me the videos. Three: let me know when we can Skype so I can see your face. Four: confirm that ticket for July."

"Yes, boss. I thought about learning French as well, in between all the chores you have for me."

"Don't worry about that now. I'll teach you when you're here."

"I need to be able to understand what you say about me to your friends and family when you introduce me. You could be saying anything."

"Perhaps, but you can rest assured they will only be good things."

Camille has a knack for always knowing the right thing to say, even from miles away. We exchange some more loved-up talk and by the time we ring off, my heart sings with glee.

CHAPTER FIFTEEN

Two weeks after Camille has left, I'm the one instigating contact with Rebecca. I finally feel ready to attempt a blameless conversation with her.

I invite her to the house, which I still haven't put on the market. I want to move to Darlinghurst, but the sense of urgency I had before I met Camille has left me. I haven't allowed any more bookings in the Airbnb. I'm not ready for that yet. Perhaps when Myrtle has finally recovered from her pneumonia and she can deal with everything again.

It's strange to let Rebecca into the house she lived in for more than a decade, but she gave me her key the night she left. I'm sure it was meant to be some sort of symbolic gesture for her, leaving the past—being me—behind. For the longest time, I left it in the spot she put it.

"God, this place," she says, and looks around as if she's seeing it for the first time. "We were happy here for a long time." She turns to me. "I'm glad you called. I need this too."

"How are things?" Without asking, I make her a cup of the chamomile tea she always drank.

"Good, I—I just worry about you. I've been meaning to get in touch after last time, but I didn't really know what to say so as not to provoke too much of a reaction."

"I've met someone," I blurt out. It feels good but also strange to say it.

"You have?" Rebecca looks as though this is a big surprise to her. As if, after she left me, I must have become the least attractive woman in Sydney. "That's great."

"It made me realize some things about why it went wrong between us." The only reason I'm able to speak to Rebecca in such a calm manner about this is because I practiced this conversation with Camille on Skype yesterday. When all you can do is talk—instead of other activities that occupy the tongue as well as the mind—you tend to spill your guts. Not being able to touch Camille has given me a clear window into her soul, and vice versa. Sometimes we talk without seeing each other. I just lie down, close my eyes, and enjoy the sound of her voice in my ear and the fact that, even though she's so far away, she can still feel so near.

"I told you before. What I did was wrong, in any respect. There's no excuse for going behind your back and not having the guts to tell you I'd met someone else. I should have made a choice sooner," Rebecca says.

"But life is not perfect like that. Things ending with one partner and seamlessly moving on to the next."

"Life is bloody messy," she says, and sends me a smile that used to drive me mad. A long time ago. "Tell me about the woman you've met."

I can't suppress a grin, then tell her all about Camille.

"Paris?" Rebecca raises her eyebrows. "Damn."

"I know. It's a bit far." I look away, past her, straight at a piece of art she acquired, but failed to take with her. When she left, it was as though she didn't need anything from the home we shared for such a long time. As though she wanted to forget all about it as quickly as possible—and about me in the process. "But I didn't ask you here to tell you all about my new relationship. That's not what this is." Although, I must admit, it does give me a certain degree of satisfaction to tell my ex I've found love again. "I guess I want you to know that..." This is hard to say. "I'm finally willing to take responsibility for my part in what went wrong between us. I let us coast along. It was enough for me, or so I believed. I was wrong."

Rebecca puts down her cup of tea and leans back on the couch. "The past couple of years, you made me feel more rejected than wanted." She looks at me from under her lashes, as though waiting for me to change my tune and blame it all on her again. She was the one who cheated after all. The obvious guilty party.

"I see that now."

"We had some serious lesbian bed death going on, and every time I tried to talk to you about it, you blew me off."

Yesterday, when I was talking to Camille about this on the phone, I had just woken up and I was still groggy with sleep. But I knew, as soon as I opened my eyes, that I wanted to be honest with her about how things ended with Rebecca. Really honest. Not the sort of honesty I'd been practicing with myself and everyone else, casting all the blame on Rebecca because it was so much easier than owning up to my own shortcomings.

"It was hard. Too hard for me, I guess," I say.

"I think, in the end, it was a clear sign we'd grown apart."

"There's a cliché phrase if ever there was one." I manage a smile.

"I don't mean it like that." Nothing about Rebecca is menacing today. She has had a lot of time to think this over as well. Actually, she's had more. Because she came to the conclusion that we were over before I did. And it hurt that she made the decision without me, but in this either, I'm not blameless.

"We both made mistakes." I clear my throat. "But truth be told, when you told me that you'd be searching elsewhere for affection if I didn't give you any some time soon, I really didn't think you meant it." I can smile at it now—a little. It wasn't even a blazing row we had when she said that. We were never the screaming-arguments-at-each-other type. We always kept it civil. Maybe too civil. Maybe we should have said what we meant more often.

"I didn't mean it. Of course, I didn't."

"Looks to me like you did." This is far more difficult than yesterday, when the words came easier, and Camille put them into immediate perspective for me. But I need to do this. Rebecca and I need to have this conversation. It's far too late for anything but closure, yet it seems to be what I need. It feels as though I must finish one chapter—the Rebecca one—before I can start on the next one with Camille.

Rebecca tilts her head. "It was a little more complicated than that and I think you know that."

"I do."

"Lots of things went wrong between us. The trouble was that it wasn't one big thing at one given time. The erosion of our relationship started so slowly, so incrementally, that we didn't even notice. We stopped communicating properly. We stopped looking forward to seeing each other after a long day at work. We stopped hanging out. We used to be so good at just being together, doing nothing special, just chatting. And because it didn't happen overnight, we barely noticed."

"And then I barely noticed when you met someone else."

"I always figured you knew but were waiting for me to say it out loud," Rebecca says.

"I guess on some level I did know, but I was afraid to confront it. I was afraid to do anything, really. In that respect, I fucked up massively."

"Relationships are complex partnerships. We were lucky. Ours ran smoothly for so long."

"Until it didn't," I say. Ever since she left, I've been trying to more closely pinpoint the time when things started going awry between us. Unlike Rebecca, I'm convinced it's not the lack of action between the sheets. I see that more as a consequence of the distance that was increasing between us. But I'm willing to try to see things from her perspective.

"I believed it would never end between us," I say on a

sigh. I glance at her and I can't help but compare her to Camille. They're not night and day exactly, but Camille's overall demeanor is much gentler, more elegant. Rebecca isn't large in body, but she is in personality. She can bulldoze anyone with one well-aimed phrase.

"For the longest time, so did I," she says. "It's the core belief of any relationship."

I clear my throat. "Is that how you feel about Julie now?" Even though I'm in the throes of falling in love myself, just speaking the other woman's name still stings.

"I never expected to fall for her the way I did." Rebecca's shoulders hunch. "It all started with the most innocent flirting."

"That's how most things start. And I've never known flirting to be innocent."

"Look, Zoya." She leans over and puts her elbows on her knees. "I know I really hurt you. And that's something I'll have to learn to live with. But it happened. And I believe it happened for a reason. For *many* reasons. I'm not asking for you to get to know her, just… give her a chance. She's not the devil."

I shake my head. "She knew you were in a committed relationship. She probably got off on it."

Now it's Rebecca's turn to shake her head. "It wasn't like that at all. It took forever for us to move on to the next step. Once we did, we were both wracked with guilt."

I hold up my hands. "I'm not sure I'm ready to hear about how it all came to be. It's none of my business, really."

"Then tell me about you and Camille. You're here and she's in Paris. How's that going to play out?" Rebecca reaches for her cup. The tea must have gone cold by now.

I think of Camille, wishing it was her sitting in Rebecca's spot on the couch. She must be waking up right now. What are her plans for the day?

"It's going to have to be long-distance. I booked a ticket to Paris for July. I'll be spending the hiatus there."

"So it's serious and you're thinking long term."

"I am. We are." I scan Rebecca's face for any signs of skepticism, but find none. "I know it will be hard but I want this to work. She's pretty amazing."

Rebecca gives a chuckle. "It's so strange to hear you talk like that about another woman. I know I have absolutely no right to say this, but it is." She puts her cup back down and looks around. "When she's here for a visit, you must introduce me."

I hope she's not waiting for me to give her permission for a formal introduction to Julie. I already know all there is to know about Julie Watson. I'm not ready for a sit-down dinner and a civilized conversation with my ex-partner's secret lover just yet.

"That might be a while." For a split second, it seems so unfair that Rebecca got to have her cake and eat it too, while all I can do is pine for Camille. But the feeling passes quickly, because if it wasn't for meeting Camille, and developing these feelings, I wouldn't even be able to sit here with Rebeca and have this conversation. And Julie's name would not be allowed to be spoken out loud in this house. Though I dread to think of the number of the times Rebecca slipped into bed with me while she was thinking of her.

"Does she have many ties in France. I mean, could she move here in the long run? Because, in all honesty, I don't see you moving to France any time soon."

"She has two children and a grandchild on the way." Camille spoke in such hopeful, sweet tones about Flo's and her visit to the gynecologist last week.

Rebecca makes a tsk-ing sound. "Very strong ties."

"We'll see what happens. No one can predict the future."

Rebecca narrows her eyes. "I know you. Better than anyone. Surely you must have thought about it."

It figures Rebecca would say something like this. Would try to throw me off the very fine balance I've found that makes our insecure future bearable.

"I have, but it's still early days. In a sense, it feels wrong to even have the audacity to think that far ahead."

"Knowing you, that wouldn't stop you. Plus, it's only logical. Human nature. Thoughts you simply can't stop."

"Camille isn't going to move her family to Australia, is she?" I say matter-of-factly.

Rebecca quirks up her eyebrows. "Wow," is all she says.

I sink my teeth into my bottom lip—something I do when I'm feeling particularly uncertain. In the end, it's the insecurity that kills me most of all. And being robbed of the opportunity to just—very simply—fall in love and get to know another woman without having to resort to the Internet and keeping time zones in mind. It's the hours that Camille is sleeping and I'm awake that are the hardest. The feeling of not being able to reach her.

"We'll see." What else can I possibly say?

"To be continued," Rebecca says and fixes her gaze on a picture on the wall to our right. "I was afraid to ask you before, but I've always liked that one." She points at it. "Any chance your state of being newly in love has left you in a sharing mood?"

"You can take anything you want." If she takes that one off my hands, I can replace it with a picture of Camille.

"How's the house sale coming along?" There's a sudden edge to her voice.

"I haven't really found an agent I'm comfortable with."

Rebecca cocks her head. "You're dragging your feet. Have you changed your mind about selling?"

I shrug. "Things are a bit up in the air right now." She's right. I have been dragging my feet.

"No rush," she says. Rebecca has always been the least materialistic person I know. When we bought the rental flat, it wasn't for the possible income it could generate, but for the joy of having a new place to fuss over and decorate. "You'll sell it some time before you move to Paris." She has a crooked grin on her face and I can't help but wonder if her words are prophetic. As ridiculous as they sound in my head, in my heart, something about them rings true.

CHAPTER SIXTEEN

Often, when it's night time in Paris and I can't sleep, I watch the videos Camille and I made. I know the interview part by heart, know every expression her face will fold into before she replies to a question. The other video has been harder to watch. The only time I managed to get through it fully was when we were simultaneously talking on Skype and we could giggle at it together—and a giggle fest it was.

I'm still not convinced any person should ever watch themselves having sex. It might be a fetish for some, but it's not for me. That much I've learned. Camille doesn't seem to have that much of a problem with it.

"It's because you're French," I told her when we were watching it and I scrutinized her face for signs of cringing.

"It's just sex, Zoya," she said. "What's more beautiful than two people enjoying themselves like that?"

"I can think of many things," I replied in mild disgust.

"Don't tell me I've gone and fallen in love with a prude." She faked a shocked expression.

"Don't tell me I've fallen in love with a woman who believes in the merits of porn."

"*Chérie,*" she said, making me melt a little. "First of all, that video of you and me is as far removed from porn as can be. Second, I actually do believe that porn can fulfill a purpose. I'd be lying if I said I don't watch it myself from time to time." All of this with a straight face, looking right into her laptop's camera.

HARPER BLISS

"You watch porn?" I thought it was pretty clear from my offended tone that I didn't.

"You mean you don't?" She grimaced. "That explains a lot."

"What's that supposed to mean?"

"It explains your reaction to our video, for starters."

"But... don't you think porn vile and exploitative of women?"

"Not always, no. I'm not naive about it. But that doesn't mean I can't enjoy it once in a while."

"So... what do you watch?"

"I've trawled through too many hours of fake lesbian porn featuring women with nails so long, you wouldn't want them anywhere near you." She chuckled. "But when you dig around a bit, you can find women-friendly videos. In which the women actually look like they're enjoying it. That usually does the trick."

"Is that how you remained a lesbian virgin for so long? By watching lesbian porn?"

She shook her head. "Not really. I have a pretty vivid imagination and I always had quite the crush on the principal at Ben's school. I was quite sad when Ben left for university because it meant I would never see her again."

I couldn't believe what I was hearing. Some things are harder to take when your partner is ten thousand miles away.

"I'm winding you up, *chérie*. You should know that by now." She sat there grinning into the camera.

I wasn't entirely convinced she was, but I managed a chuckle anyway.

I try to watch the video again—trying to be less of a prude. Trying not to tie it into how Rebecca sometimes accused me of not wanting to attempt anything too new in bed and spice things up. But Camille's joking comment continues to give me pause. Maybe I *am* a bit of a prude. Maybe it's just my nature.

When I focus on Camille only, my pulse quickens a

little. I can bear the sight of my hand on her breast, but anything more of me and my arousal plummets. Maybe matters would be helped if I watched something that didn't involve me. Two strangers going at it. If it works for Camille, perhaps it can work for me.

I type *lesbians making love* into Google and am instantly confronted with a barrage of naked women in variations of being all over each other. It reminds me of Rebecca suggesting we watch porn together once, a long time ago. I laughed her comment away. Christ, I really am a prude—and I wasn't even raised Catholic. That's what Rebecca used to say to me. "All that guilt and you're not even a Catholic." She would then shake her head and make a tutting sound. "Good thing you're not Irish like me because our relationship might have remained purely platonic."

I click on one of the videos and instantly recognize the opposite of what Camille claimed to enjoy. These women are not into this at all. That's all I see. Two women pretending. Do men really fall for this? Is that really all it takes? It doesn't do anything for me. Maybe I should ask Camille for advice on where to look, seeing as she's such an expert. I might surprise her after all.

In comparison, the expression on Camille's face while I was fucking her is much more enticing. The pure ecstasy displayed in her entire posture—and the way she looks into the camera after.

When does she wake up again? When she just returned from Australia and was suffering from a massive bout of jet lag, she would wake so early, we could chat for an hour before she had to leave for work, but as time has gone by and her body has adjusted to the French time zone, our—for her — morning chats have become shorter and shorter and have now, almost a month later, dwindled to nothing. Turns out she's not much of a morning person after all. Something I can hardly hold against her.

I close all tabs on my computer and check my phone.

No messages. She's not awake yet. I'll have to exercise more patience.

———

The next time we Skype it's the weekend and we can luxuriate in a long chat.

"Guess where I'm going tonight?" Camille asks me after we've exchanged our habitual silly string of *I-miss-yous* and *I-wish-you-were-heres*.

"Hm." I pretend to think really hard about this, even though she tends to make me guess every day she has something on and I never do, because I don't know her friends and her going-out habits well enough to predict or see a pattern just yet. I know all about her best friends Sylvie and Sébastien, with whom she spends a lot of time during the weekend. And Flo's parents-in-law whom she's always gotten along with very well. "You're doing a cabaret show at le Moulin Rouge?" I joke.

"Close." She sends me a smile. "I'm going to a MLR event and the president of our troubled republic is rumored to make an appearance."

"What?" I fake indignation in my voice. "You're going to have a chat with Dominique Laroche while all I get to do for my Saturday evening entertainment is chat with you."

"I know. Tough break for you." She sends me a faux apologetic grin. "But… we could do more than chat, I guess."

"What do you mean?" I ask, even though I know very well what she means. She's been hinting at it, and I've been pretty receptive to the idea, taking her hints not only in jest, but giving her a genuine reply at more regular intervals. Still, that video we made plays in my head every time the subject comes up.

"*Allez, chérie,*" she says. "*Tu sais.*" You know.

"All right. If I understand correctly, you would like to engage in some Internet sex just to take the edge off for when you find yourself in the magnetic presence of your president."

"That's exactly it, yes. You know me so well." She purses her lips. "I want to see you, Zoya." Already, when she says my name in an imploring manner like that, I know she wants something really badly. She can't hide the desire in her voice. "*Really* see you."

"Me too." My tone is suddenly serious.

"Good." Her smile is sweet and seductive.

"How does it work?" I know it makes me sound overly naive. And it's not as if Camille is well-versed in long-distance relationship protocols. We're figuring this out as we go along, together.

"I imagine we find a comfortable place where we won't be disturbed." She looks down. "Which, in my case, means I'll need to get a pussycat off my lap."

I chuckle. I'm already lying in bed, though I am still fully dressed.

"Then you'll have to strip for me because you must already be in a sultrier evening mood and I may need a bit more enticing to get my juices flowing." She sits there grinning again. "What with it still being so early here."

"Ten in the morning is hardly the crack of dawn."

"It's been a bit of a crazy week." She pretends to stifle a yawn.

"Don't I know it." Apparently, the French like to engage in many after-work drinks and dinners during the week. After having been away for two months, Camille has many people to see. While I have to drag myself back out there and pick up my life where I left it post-Rebecca. Maybe now that we're back on sort-of speaking terms, I should see some of our mutual friends who knew about Rebecca's affair and failed to tell me. Right after the break up, in my head, I had put them into her camp immediately and refused to speak to them when they reached out.

"Give me a few minutes while I change rooms." She blows a kiss into the camera and I hear an offended meow as she shoos Iris off her lap. The screen gets blurry as Camille walks to her bedroom, of which I've gotten as detailed a tour as a laptop camera allows.

While I wait, anticipation hums in my blood. I won't have to look at myself on the screen. With a few clicks I can make the little rectangle with my image disappear completely and only focus on Camille. As long as we're not recording this.

"Hey," she says, her head resting on an upturned palm. It looks like she's lying on her side. "I'm ready for my striptease now."

"You were serious about that?"

She just smiles and says nothing. I'm not really in the mood to start stripping just yet.

"Talk to me," I say, wishing I had control over the zoom function of her camera and I could let my lens swoop over her body the way that I see fit, letting my focus slide from one area to the next—feeling a little more in control than I do now.

"I want to see you, Zoya," she repeats. Her tone has gained intensity. "Please." With a soft smile on her lips, she starts to unbutton her blouse. It's a linen one of which she seems to have an endless supply in pastel colors. "I want you to see me," she continues. "As soon as we log off Skype, it's all I think about. I've barely been back for a month, but that video isn't cutting it anymore. I need something more and new to tide me over until I can hold you in my arms again."

"How many more days?" I ask, even though I know the number. I repeat it ceaselessly throughout the day. It's the first thing I think of when I wake up, when I have subtracted another night from the time keeping us apart.

"Thirty-three," she says, her voice so sultry she makes it sound like a dirty word.

Camille shrugs out of her blouse. She's not wearing a bra. The sight of her naked chest is all I need to spur me on to uncover myself. I clumsily drag my top over my head, not caring about removing garments in a sexy way. Camille has pushed her body away from the camera a bit, so more of her is visible, and the sight of her wearing just jeans and nothing else is too thrilling for me to care much for decorum.

"That's my favorite outfit on you," I say with a husky voice.

"Yeah? Should I go out in it tonight? Cause a scandal?" She chuckles and flips open her jeans button. "I'm waiting." Her hand remains on her crotch, not moving.

I unhook my bra and let my breasts spill free. It feels so different to do it while she's watching me, even more so because she's watching me on a laptop from so many miles away.

"I want to touch you," she says. Everything about her face tells me she's deadly serious.

Instinctively, I start thinking of ways to make it possible. But she's simply too far away for a quick weekend rendezvous. Since starting my show ten years ago, I've fallen ill one single time. My voice had totally gone and there was no way I could appear on television. I was hastily replaced by a news anchor, but it's not advisable to have the host of The Zoya Das Show replaced by someone else too often. Which is one of the reasons why, over the decade that I've done the show, I've started insisting on shorter seasons as time has progressed. Making the show is intense and being ready for an energy-draining interview every week takes a toll on the mind and the body. To such an extent that I always feel a little sorry for the guests we have booked for the last episodes of the season, because by then, I'm usually so exhausted I can't help but give them a little less of myself.

To even think about taking a week off for a quick visit to France is inconceivable. Although the thought has entered my mind. But I adore my job and consider myself fortunate that the network has kept faith in me during the turmoil in TV land of the last few years. I couldn't possibly feign illness to hop over to France to see my girlfriend. This comes with the job, of course. A job I'm well paid for and get to take a couple of months off from every year.

So when I say, "Me too" to Camille, I mean it from the bottom of my heart but I say it with the full knowledge that there's absolutely nothing I can do about it.

"Touch yourself for me," she says. "I will feel it."

I believe her.

I slip out of my jeans and sit in front of my laptop wearing just underwear. No, I sit in front of Camille in lingerie. There. That sounds entirely different.

And it's not as if I haven't touched myself numerous times since she left, pretending she was watching me. In a way, this is just another fantasy coming true. But the distance between fantasy and reality is hard to bridge sometimes, so I do feel awkward when I hook my thumbs underneath my panties and slide them over my legs. Baring myself to her.

It also feels surprisingly exhilarating, just like this entire journey with Camille has been.

I glance at the screen, at Camille's transfixed face. She's still wearing her jeans, which seems highly unfair to me. I want to see her just as much.

I tilt my head and she snaps to attention. "I only see half of you," she says in a husky tone. "You'll need to reposition your laptop."

"And you'll need to take your jeans off." I can't keep a smile out of my voice. Despite the exhilaration, there's an air of ludicrousness to this situation that keeps me teetering on the brink of hysterical laughter.

"I think the best angle would be achieved if you placed the camera between your legs, but not too close," she says, ignoring my remark about disrobing more.

"So much for foreplay," I protest, refusing to be directed in this way from so many miles away.

Camille giggles. "I'm sorry. I got a little sidetracked by your nakedness. I just... really want to see all of you. It's been driving me crazy." In between the giggles, I can hear the desperation in her voice. A sentiment I fully sympathize with. I drive myself crazy with thoughts of her at least once every day.

"Okay. I'll do it." In this moment, this is all I can give her. This is what the first months of our relationship are reduced to. Two women trying to figure out the best angle for their laptop's camera in order to have successful Skype sex.

"Me too." I watch her wiggle out of her jeans and panties and instantly understand her urgency from before. Seeing her like that has the exact same effect on me.

When we finally do lie down, each on our respective ends of the world, laptop perched on a bunch of pillows near our ankles, I can really only see her chin, but I see so many other things as well. I see Camille's hands caressing her breasts, playing with her nipples, trailing along her belly button and, finally, resting at the apex of her thighs.

And, oh, does that sight arouse me. Even though I can only see her neck and chin, it's so unmistakably her. I would recognize those hands anywhere. The curve of her belly. The way she spreads her legs a little asymmetrically, with her left knee never managing to fall as deeply as her right.

I knead my own breasts and seeing her like that, and lying here in this position, does have the strange effect on me that when my hands touch my own skin, I can almost believe it's her touching me. Because we're doing this together. This is the kind of intimacy we can share across the many miles of distance.

Camille runs one finger delicately over her nether lips and my nipples harden at the sight. I'm perplexed by my rapidly growing levels of arousal. I bring my own hand down and mirror her movements, as though she's guiding me, wordlessly telling me what to do with myself.

Camille seems to have a nose for these things, a knack for drawing me out of my own prudish self the way Rebecca never could. Maybe it's because she's French, though that seems a bit simplistic. She's many, many more things than French, though, silly as it may sound, the fact that she is adds to her allure.

Camille circles her finger around her clit and as she does I wish I had a bigger screen. I wish I had pushed the record button so I could zoom in later.

I follow her lead and am in for another surprise when I circle my own clit. The touch shoots through me like an arrow of lust was shot straight from her house in Paris and traveled all the way to Sydney at an unimaginable speed.

My finger remains glued to my clit as I watch Camille stroke herself. She might be putting on a show for me when she lets two fingers slip inside of herself and utters a slight moan. Whatever her intentions, what she's doing is not missing its effect, because I feel compelled to increase the speed at which my finger circles my clit. The vision of Camille's own fingers fucking her is, by far, the most arousing thing I've ever seen. I make a mental note to ask her to do so when we're physically together, curious about the effect it would have on me then. Maybe the fact that I'm enjoying it so much right now is inexorably connected to this particular situation. To her being so far away and us trying to create closeness by doing this. Maybe the lust traveling through me right now is helped by the lack of proximity because I'm not sure I could do this with her in the room, whether I could reach this stage of abandon.

But I do now. Camille lets her fingers slip out and even that action ratchets up my arousal. She starts circling her clit again, only for a few rounds, then brings her fingers back inside. My breathing is ragged and my clit throbs against my fingertip. I increase my rhythm and I can feel myself slipping over the edge. My eyes are glued to the screen, to the image of Camille's fingers inside herself—an image so arresting I will remember it forever. Then I experience another first. I come while staring at a laptop screen, while engaging in Internet sex with my long-distance lover. The climax is quick but intense and exhilarating because of its surprise factor.

I see Camille's body jerking a little on the screen. Seeing me come has pushed her over her very own edge as well. Her hands lie limp between her legs and I hear a chuckle burst through the speaker.

When we've repositioned our laptops and can see each other's faces properly again, Camille has a triumphant smirk on her face.

"Did you like that?" she asks coyly. Clearly, she already knows the answer.

But I'm in no mood to be coy myself. I'm engulfed by passion and love, still reeling from that unexpected bout of horniness and delight running through me at the mere sight of her. "It was wonderful," I say, my voice sweet as honey.

"Same time next week?" she asks, the grin wiped off her face.

"Oh yes." We lie naked on our beds chatting for two hours after.

CHAPTER SEVENTEEN

Weeks pass and even though my life is tinted by the shiny new gloss of falling in love, I fail to find my groove. In between work, of which the hours seem to extend as the season draws nearer to its close, composing emails to Camille, skyping with Camille at often ungodly hours, and keeping a semblance of a social life, I fail to make any decisions about putting the house on the market and starting the process of moving to Darlinghurst. It seems as though, subconsciously, something is stopping me from taking the next step away from my former life. It's not because of Rebecca, with whom I'll never be friends even though our interactions have grown more civilized. Rebecca is not the type of person to push me on the house. She's not waiting for the money from the sale. And she has already moved on.

It feels as though I've become incapable of following through on the decision to move away from Balmain. Somewhere in the back of my brain, the thought rests that it would be futile to take a big step like moving house and neighborhood right now. There's too much turmoil going on in my mind and, even though I'm not willing to admit this to myself out loud, I feel like I need to keep my mind clear to focus on another, more important decision.

Because I regularly find myself staring at my reflection in the mirror and asking myself why I'm doing this. Yes, of course, the practicalities of my life don't allow me to see Camille in France. And the same goes for her. The distance we harbor between us is too vast for many things, but it isn't for the love I feel for her and the way it multiplies in magnitude and force every single day. Some nights, when I can't sleep because my mind is too wound up thinking about her and trying to come up with creative ways to bridge the distance, all I can think of is the moment we'll finally be together again. How it will make me feel. To wake up next to her every day. Go to sleep kissing her goodnight. And I ask myself which sacrifices I'm willing to make. If the time comes—and if my visit to Paris goes well—would I be willing to make the ultimate one? Would I be willing to leave Australia? Start a new life in France—a country where I can't even speak the language?

In the dead of night, darkness all around me, when my decision doesn't carry much weight, my answer is always an astoundingly easy *yes*. Because I know that a woman like Camille only comes along every so often. I'm forty-seven. For me, she might be the last one to ever present herself the way she did. Cocking a smile and seizing my heart in the process.

Even though we only spent six days in each other's physical presence, there's no doubt in my mind I want to be with her. But the sacrifice would be real and great. If I move to France, I would need to start from scratch. The career I've built in Sydney wouldn't mean a thing. I'd be jobless. I haven't been without a job since I left university. What would I possibly do with myself all day? Let love fill my hours? I'm not as naive to think that romance can take the place of professional satisfaction. And with these thoughts, I am alone. It would feel too ridiculous to talk about this with Caitlin, although her and Josephine's relationship seems to have progressed rather quickly as well. But it's not the same. Because they live in the same city and the same country. Camille and I do not.

I also don't dare breach the subject with Camille. And, in a way, it's funny that the only person I've talked to about this briefly is my ex. Because she knows me and she knows the way I think.

But ever since Camille left, even though her visit to Australia was short, I feel like something big—the biggest thing possible—is missing. I don't have children to distract me with tales of their life and grandchildren to care for. My family is in Perth and even though we talk regularly, I don't see them very often and we don't have the kind of close relationship where I feel I need to show up every other month for a weekend with them.

Most nights, when I lie in bed pining for Camille, it feels like I don't have much to stay for at all. But I know that if I keep mulling this over in my head, without taking the pressure off by saying the words out loud to someone, I will drive myself crazy sooner rather than later. So when I meet Caitlin for coffee at the Pink Bean after leaving work early one day, I'm glad neither Micky nor Josephine are present, and I can spill my heart to her without snarky interruptions.

"How many more days, my friend?" Caitlin asks after she has given me a lingering hug. She has taken to asking me this question after she overheard me and Camille signing off on a phone call. "You look like you can't go on much longer without a healthy dose of your French lover."

"Twenty-one," I say on a sigh. "It feels more like twenty-one years."

"You will come back, won't you?" She narrows her eyes then flashes a smile.

"I have to. I present a show that is named after me." I sigh again.

Caitlin quirks up her eyebrows. "Jesus. You make it sound all exciting." She leans over the table. "Just off the top of my head, I can think of at least five men at ANBC who would happily bump you off your Saturday night prime time throne and present a show that is named after *them*."

"Don't I know it." Traditionally, female newscasters are preferred to brighten up breakfast shows or present the news, not do the type of interviewing I do on television. The fact that I've been doing it for ten years straight doesn't sit right with quite a few men who still believe a woman's place is elsewhere. "But I just want the season to be over. I always get tired as July approaches, but this year, it's different. It's not just fatigue. I've always loved this job, every aspect of it, but lately it has been feeling more like a burden. Like a cage around my freedom. Look at you, Caitlin. You could pick up your life and decide to spend six months in another country at the drop of a hat. You even did it. You lived in the US for so long, decided to come back and did so, because you could. If you wanted to, you could reinvent yourself in another place all over again."

"You're in love. It's normal for your priorities to shift." She glances at her coffee. "I feel like we should have had this conversation in a bar rather than a coffee shop."

"I just miss her. And it sounds stupid, but really, it's the thought that occupies my mind the most. I just miss her. And it makes me feel all sorts of inadequate but at the same time, the thought of her also fills me with hope and love. I don't want to sit here feeling sorry for myself, because look at me? I have it all. But when you look a little closer, I don't really. And everything just feels so screwed up in my head."

"You've been through a lot. First your break-up from Rebecca and all that put you through. All the while needing your focus on a demanding job. Then having to say goodbye to Camille. It's okay to feel the way you do. You can express as much self-pity to me as you like."

I wave her off. "Nobody wants to listen to their friends complain all the time."

"Well, I'm telling you that I don't mind listening to you." She shoots me a warm smile.

"Thanks." I stare out of the window for a second. "It's only twenty-one days now and it's already so hard. Say everything goes well in Paris. I stay with Camille for two months and we fall deeper in love. Then I have to come home and I can't go back for another nine or ten months."

"She can come here."

"Can she?"

"Why not? She can take a few weeks off work."

"Sure, a few weeks."

"What are you really trying to say?" Caitlin asks.

"I've been thinking about taking a sabbatical." I glance at her from under my lashes. "Don't I get to go on my *Eat, Pray, Love* journey?"

Caitlin pins her gaze on me. "Of course, but just don't make any rash decisions. Go to Paris first. See how things go."

"But that's just the thing about my job. I can't just come back from Paris, call up Jack, and ask him for a year off. It'll be too late by then."

Caitlin shakes her head. "You don't know that." She pulls her lips into a smile. "From what I've learned in my long and prosperous life, there's usually a solution to every problem."

I quirk up my eyebrows. "I know for a fact you're only saying that to cheer me up. There have been plenty of situations that didn't have an easy way out."

"I never said it would be easy. You just have to think outside of the box a little."

"What are you trying to say?" I get the distinct feeling this conversation is no longer only about me.

"There are always options." She leans back in her chair. "Say you come back from Paris and want to go back the next month for an extended period. This could happen. I mean, it could also not happen, but let's say things play out that way. How about you, Jack and the network come to an easy agreement on who to replace you with for the time you're away. And I'd like to stress the word *easy*." She sits there grinning coyly.

The penny drops as I stare at the triumphant expression on her face.

I start smiling too, not so much because of the possibly elegant solution Caitlin has come up with, but mostly because of the sheer audacity of it. "I didn't know one of my best friends had her eyes on my job." I'm not sure whether I should feel thankful or threatened.

"I don't. The idea just came to me. But the more I think about it, the more it excites me."

"Is this because you fear your girlfriend might become more successful than you? You want a regular primetime spot on national television?"

Her mouth drops open for a split second, then she recovers. "Firstly, I'm trying to do you a favor here. I know Jack is quite fond of me and the network doesn't seem too averse to me either. Secondly, this has nothing to do with Josephine."

"I'm sorry. I shouldn't have said that."

She waves me off. "Ah, you're in a state. It's true that she has been very busy lately. And she refuses to move in with me, so I don't get to see her as often as I would like."

"She's young. She needs her independence."

"What she needs most of all is more hours in her day." Caitlin's voice isn't scornful, just a little melancholic.

"Don't we all." I throw up my hands. "You would, if you wanted to present The Zoya Das Show."

"We'd have to temporarily rename it The Caitlin James Show, of course." She chuckles.

"You'd have to interview a few people you don't like very much. I'm not sure you can be trusted to treat them with the necessary respect required on TV."

She slants her head. "I never said it would be easy."

"You're quite something, Caitlin."

"All I'm trying to say is that if you need a woman—a friend—to keep your seat warm, I'm up for it. Details are for later. I just want you to have some peace of mind and not walk around in Paris worrying about your job. In the end, it's just a job. It's a lucrative and prestigious one, I won't argue against that, but it is just a job. Other things are more important."

"Thanks for the motivational minute." It's easy to say for Caitlin, who has always had something else to fall back on —all careers she built for herself. But I do appreciate the message she's trying to send. It's her way of saying everything will be okay and things will fall into place as they tend to do. "Are you sure you and Jo are okay?"

She doesn't speak for a few seconds. "We're fine. We really are. But it seems that the dynamic of our relationship is changing rather quickly."

"In a good way?"

"I've always believed that as long as there's respect, there is no bad way." She falls silent again. Perhaps she's not ready to talk about it yet. Knowing Caitlin, she'll tell me all about it when she is. She refocuses her gaze on me. "Twenty-one days until you get an in with Dominique Laroche. Have you come up with a strategy yet?"

"President Laroche is the least of my worries. All my thoughts are preoccupied with one woman."

CHAPTER EIGHTEEN

Twenty-one days later, I'm finally on the plane. My flight follows a different route than Camille's, with the longest journey to Doha first, followed by a slightly shorter one to Charles de Gaulle Airport in France.

I can't quite believe I'm on my way to see her. But when the plane takes off, and I'm flying in the direction of Camille, all the pent-up emotion breaks free and I burst into inadvertent tears.

A member of the cabin crew rushes to my side, asking whether I'm all right.

"Just a bit emotional," I mumble. "Nothing to worry about."

When she's gone, I wonder whatever I'm going to do with myself for the next twenty-odd hours in this cabin in the sky. Drinking is an option, but I want to arrive in Paris looking the best I can. Even though I've waited two months to board this plane, these last few days have been the hardest. Time seemed to slow down more and more as my departure time approached. On top of that, Camille hasn't been that reachable because four weeks ago she became a grandmother to a baby girl named Emma and she's been spending most of her free time helping out her daughter.

I'm not one to be jealous of a newborn baby, but sharing the spotlight of Camille's heart with someone new from all those miles away has presented me with an extra challenge. There was an unexpected benefit though. A few days after Flo was allowed to leave the hospital, Camille Skyped me from her daughter's house and formally introduced me to Flo, Mathieu, and Emma. It was a significant moment in our relationship.

Soon, I'll be meeting them all in the flesh. *Soon.* First I have a flight to get through. And it's a flight unlike any other I've been on before. Not because of my fellow passengers and not even because of the destination—it's not my first trip to Paris—but because of all the emotions that lie in wait for me when I arrive.

It feels like I'm traveling toward a new life. Even though there's also the anxiety of not really knowing what is going to happen when I see Camille again. When I spend time with her on her turf. When she tries to integrate me into her everyday life and introduces me to her family and friends.

Two months of anticipation make me ask for a double gin and tonic after takeoff and I eagerly wait for the alcohol to hit my bloodstream and relax my frantic mind. Despite Camille's insistence that these days anyone can get around Paris perfectly well only speaking English and that she would teach me all the French I need, I've purchased a French language course. I'm meant to repeat the words, but I feel a bit silly saying words I can't even pronounce out loud on an airplane, so I only repeat them in my head, probably not helping myself and my learning progress much.

After the stopover in Doha, which is short and swift and a welcome break to stretch my legs, I manage to fall asleep, images of Camille and, for some reason, Rebecca haunting my stunted dreams. By the time I land, I'm groggy and disoriented—and not much more fluent in French than when I left. It seems to take ages for the luggage to arrive, but by that time I have received eight text messages from Camille telling me she has arrived, she's waiting for me, and will I hurry up and make it into the arrivals hall.

And, then I do. In my tired mind, it happens in slow motion. I go through customs with nothing to declare except an insuppressible smile on my face. I walk through the open doors and scan the crowd. Then there she is. She's holding up a sign that says *Madame Zoya Das*. It makes me snicker, then it makes me tear up. All the built-up anticipation that has been growing for weeks and reached its peak on the long journey over here releases at the sight of Camille. Of her beautiful fingers clutching the piece of paper and her gorgeous face peeking out over the top. My eyes fill with tears as I bridge the last few steps that separate us. I stand in front of her for a split second, unable to move or say anything. Then it all bursts loose. It all comes together. I feel the conclusion bubble up right from the center of my heart. I love her. This is right. Camille and I, we're meant to be.

The sheet of paper with my name on it gets crumpled as we fall into each other's arms. I hug Camille as if I never want to let her go again. Her scent in my nose, her flesh pressed against mine. She peppers kisses on my neck and cheek.

"I thought you would never come out of that door," she whispers in my ear. "I couldn't believe you were here until I actually saw you."

"I'm here." I hold her a little tighter. "I'm here for six whole weeks."

"Let's not waste a minute of them." She holds her head back for an instant, looks at me, cups my jaw in her hands, then kisses me ever so softly on the lips. "Come on."

Charles de Gaulle airport is a mess. Camille is so elated she doesn't immediately remember where she parked her car, and once she does, and I'm sitting in the passenger seat next to her, it takes forever for the queue of cars we're in to make it out of the parking lot and off the airport premises. While Camille utters the occasional expletive—I think—in French and throws her hands in the air in exasperation, there's no room in my heart for frustration or road rage. I'm in a car with her. She's taking me to her house. I'm here for a month and a half. I haven't been to Paris since Rebecca and I celebrated our tenth anniversary. I'm ready to make some new memories here, with the new woman in my life. All the time I've had to wait, which seemed like decades while I was doing the actual waiting, seems to have dissolved into nothing, a mere speck in the course of my life, because the reward of being with Camille is so big, it obliterates the tiniest negative emotion I carry inside me.

I have no idea what time it is. The dashboard clock says 9:18 but it doesn't feel like it could possibly be nine in the morning. It doesn't matter. One look at how Camille navigates us through the bumper-to-bumper traffic onto the *périphérique* is enough for fatigue and jet lag to become distant notions, small nuisances that hold no meaning in this brand new, dazzling universe I just walked into.

Camille talks and talks, her accent more pronounced than when I met her in Sydney. She chatters about her one-month old granddaughter Emma and how she can't wait to introduce me to her family, but this first weekend will be only for us. No one else is allowed inside her house except her cat and me. She has instructed Flo to only call her in case of extreme emergencies.

"Obviously, I didn't want to spell out to my daughter what her mother was going to do all weekend long." She looks at me and waggles her eyebrows suggestively. "But I think she got the picture nonetheless." She chuckles and shrugs.

"Ben's in Provence with a bunch of his university friends," she says. "They're staying in the house we used to go to every summer when Jean-Claude and I were still together. I'd like to take you there. Show you all aspects of my life."

"I would love that." I stare at her while she's driving. It's the first time I've seen Camille behind the wheel and she looks different, but also very much the same as the day I met her. Endlessly capable of getting things done. A confidence about her that says a flat battery in a smoke detector is the least of her worries. The assured air of all the mothers I know who are not fazed by the small things in life. Except for traffic. That does seem to bother her, whereas her reaction to it amuses me greatly.

"*Connard.*" She lays on the horn. "Did you see how that *abruti* cut me off?" She turns her face to me.

I can't help but burst out laughing. "Remember that phone call in Sydney when I was stuck in traffic?"

"I'll never forget." From the look on her face, she seems to have forgotten about the *connard*—another word to add to my expanding French swear word vocabulary—who cut her off.

"Maybe you should think about that while you drive," I suggest.

"Thoughts are no longer enough now that you're here." She puts a hand on my knee. "Which is why I want to get us home as quickly as possible."

I nod my understanding, relishing the simple touch of her hand on my knee.

CHAPTER NINETEEN

I whistle through my teeth when Camille pulls up to the driveway of her house.

"I know what you're thinking," she says. "This is a politician's house, not a civil servant's."

"I was thinking no such thing." I stare at the limestone facade, the ornate front door, and the sheer size of the place.

"I inherited this house from my grandparents. Jean-Claude had no claims to make on it when we divorced. Now that the kids have flown the nest, it is admittedly a bit big for just me, but I love it here."

"I can't wait to see the inside."

"What are we waiting for then?" She leans over, brings her cool hand to the back of my neck, and slips her tongue inside my mouth. With her other hand, she opens the car door on my side.

I smile and as soon as she draws away from me I pull her closer again, kissing her.

"In case you hadn't noticed, this is a posh neighborhood. Two women kissing in a car will be heavily frowned upon," Camille says with a wide smile plastered across her face.

"I'm so very, very sorry. I wouldn't want to traumatize your neighbors and put any ideas in their head about the decent woman who lives on their street." I suck my bottom lip into my mouth.

Camille's face goes serious. "Inside. Now," she says, her

tone all intention and gravitas. She leads by example and gets out of the car, fetches my suitcase from the trunk and wheels it inside.

If the outside of the house was impressive, the inside is even more so. I always believed the house Rebecca and I lived in was majestic, but it pales in comparison to the grandeur of this place. And we've only made it to the entrance. I must ask Camille about her grandparents some time.

"Do you want coffee, tea, or just me?" Camille throws her arms around me again. "Also, just for your information, I intend to let go of you as little as possible in the coming six weeks. You'd better get used to having me glued to your skin at all times."

"No need," I whisper back. "I'm used to it already and I wouldn't have it any other way." I kiss her on the lips. "To answer your question: I think I'll just have you." The heat I grew so familiar with after meeting Camille in Sydney is rapidly making its way from the depths of my body to the surface of my skin. As exhilarating as it has been to lay eyes on her again, to see her in the flesh, and kiss her on the lips, I need more, and I need it now.

"Come on." She takes my hand and leads me up the wide staircase. I follow her and get a good look at her shapely behind while she heads up the stairs in front of me. Oh, to have my hands all over her again after all this time.

She opens one of many doors and we stand in the bathroom. "Bath or shower?" she asks.

"Whichever is most easy for you to join me." I sling an arm around her waist.

"That's a question I've never given any thought to at all. Let's take a minute to think this through."

"How about you put your scientist brain to rest and hop into the shower with me? A bath takes too long to run."

"I'm easily convinced today." She stands in front of me. "But promise me we will test both in the weeks to come."

I nod and start unbuttoning my wrinkled, traveled-in

blouse.

"Oh no." Camille puts a hand over mine. "That's my job now." While she stares into my eyes, she undoes the buttons and guides the blouse off my shoulders.

Once she's done, I pull hers from the waistband of her jeans and try to unbutton it, but my fingers seem so much less graceful than hers, or perhaps it's the brand of blouse she's wearing which comes with annoying French buttons that are impossible for a lover to undo swiftly.

Camille doesn't say anything, just starts from the top while I work from the bottom and soon enough our hands meet somewhere in the middle and her blouse is a crumpled item of clothing on the bathroom floor as well.

Once our torsos are almost naked, the rest of our clothing is removed with much more haste. As if seeing each other in bras and jeans has pushed some button in our mind and spurred us to action. No more time for words or hesitations or negotiations. I can only speak for myself, of course, but I want Camille's hands all over me in that glitzy walk-in shower with its marble walls and dozen settings. When I look into her eyes, I do think I can speak for her as well, because I see my own desire reflected back at me. And the notion that what we felt for each other in Sydney might have just been the result of a holiday romance, a fleeting fling and nothing more serious, leaves my brain forever.

Camille hops in first and turns on the tap. I follow her and soon we're standing underneath a deliciously strong jet of hot water.

Camille holds my hands and says, "I've missed you." The cascading water drowns out the sound a bit, but I can still hear her clearly. "I'm so glad you're here." Then she pulls me close and our naked bodies meet and everything is immediately different than when we hugged at the airport or even in the hallway. Two months of not being able to touch each other are concentrated in that embrace and the entire expanse of my skin starts to tingle. And I know I won't be able to wait until after this shower.

"I want you," I whisper in her ear.

"You've got me," she whispers back, and I know I do. I don't just know with a certainty bordering on insanity that she's about to make me come like I've never done before in my life, but I know I have her in many other ways as well. I have her love, her patience, her devotion only to me.

I feel her hands do something behind my back, and when we break from our soaked hug, I see the soap in her cupped hands. She cracks a crooked smile, and says, "You have no idea how many times I dreamed of this moment."

I think I do. Of course, I do, but I don't say anything. I just feel how she lathers my breasts with soap, her fingertips lingering on my nipples. She spends so much time on washing my chest, I'm compelled to remind her I do have other body parts, but it feels so divine to have her hands caress me like that, I never want her to stop.

When her hands do finally travel down my belly, I'm not sure of how long I can remain standing on my legs. Her fingers are between my legs, not probing, just stroking—washing me—but when a finger inadvertently skates along my clit my knees buckle.

"Please," I murmur.

"Not long now," she says, puts her hands on my hips, and turns me around. I have my back to her and I put my hands against the wall for support. I feel her fingers stroke my shoulders and my back and glide all the way down to my ass, spending more than their fair share of time there.

By the time she spins me back around, I'm ready to crash to the floor, lie on the cold marble, and have her do with me whatever she wants. I can't remember a time when I felt so much like putty in another person's hands. And here I stand, in a shower in a house in Neuilly, Paris' fanciest suburb, trembling under the touch of a woman I didn't even know six months ago, when I was too busy wallowing in post-break-up misery to even conjure up the thought of something like this ever being possible again.

I look into Camille's eyes. Her hair is glued to her scalp and, because it's wet, comes to her shoulders. I look at her and spread my legs instinctively because my body knows this is the time. Camille inches closer, looks back at me, and brings her hand between my legs. Then she enters me. The pure bliss that engulfs me is much more than just a physical sensation. It's a sense of coming home to a place I've never been before. Of reuniting with a woman who is in my bones. Who is in the fabric of my very being despite only having known her for a few months. It's the knowledge that between us everything just feels so right and it did so from the get-go. Maybe not from the very first minute we met, but certainly not long after.

Camille fucks me and even though it's only her two fingers touching me, I feel it everywhere. Most of all, I feel it in my soul, or whatever part of me is being moved to tears by her fucking me with all her intention, with all that love on display in her eyes.

She brings her other hand between my legs as well and positions her thumb right above my swollen clit. Every time her fingers thrust up high inside me, making my breath hitch in my throat—every time she makes me hers a little more—her thumb brushes against my clit and I lose myself a fraction more. The fractions add up and soon I am panting at her fingertips, wholly at her mercy, waiting for the exhilarating heat that's building in my core to spread through my body, for my clenched-up muscles to release, for the climax that's been building for months to rip through me and leave me spent in Camille's arms.

Camille doesn't speed up the rhythm of her fingers inside of me, but she does amp up the intensity. I feel her more. It feels as though, in this shower, we're sealing our fate. Six weeks of this, I think, as I crash underneath the wave of my orgasm. As I cry out her name, dig my nails into her flesh, ride out my climax on her magnificent fingers. Six weeks of heaven.

"You're so much more beautiful in real life," she whispers when I come to, when words start making sense again. "Especially naked with my fingers inside of you." Her voice is hoarse, shot through with raw desire.

"I love you." I bring my hands to her cheeks and pull her close, kiss her as deeply as I can, wanting her all over me all over again.

When we break from our kiss, it's my turn to put her against the wall. I kiss her from the lips down to her collar bone and breasts. Then I kneel in front of her, ignoring the hardness of the floor against my knees, and bring my lips between her legs. My hands dig into the soft flesh of her behind, I pull her to me and drink her in. I lick and suck and taste the fruit that has been denied to me for so long and as I do, I know, I already know for certain in that moment, that I will never spend this long apart from her again. I don't know how or when, because details don't matter when it comes to instinct and love at first sight.

CHAPTER TWENTY

When I wake up the next day, after my first twenty-four hours in Paris have been filled with sex, hugs, and the pure joy of being together, I can hardly believe that I get to throw my arms around Camille as soon as I open my eyes. After she left Sydney, the mornings were always the hardest because they were the beginning of another day without her. A day I had to start with an empty spot in my bed. A day that didn't take off with me wrapping myself around her, looking into her eyes and, just because of that, knowing it would be a good one.

Camille is still sleeping but I have to touch her. I can't be in this bed with her, fully awake, and not feel her skin against mine. Not after all the abstinence of touch we've had to endure. She doesn't stir when I run a finger over her arm, or when my embrace grows more intense and I curl an arm around her waist, my fingers crawling to her sex—as though they can't help themselves.

Even though she's still asleep, the intimacy of the moment floors me. I bury my nose in her hair and inhale her smell. How can it be? I ask myself. How can I be so smitten with this woman? At the end-of-season party for the show, to which I invited Jason, he gave me a book called *The Brain in Love* and said, "For on the plane." I didn't even bring it. It's gathering dust in my house in Sydney, because I didn't want to read the scientific explanation of what is happening to me —to my brain. Even though right now, I'd like to consult it to find out why it feels so much like the most exquisite insanity imaginable.

Then Camille turns around in my embrace, her warm, naked body sliding against mine, and I no longer care about the theories of falling in love. It's all practicalities for me now that we've been reunited.

"What time is it?" she asks, her accent so thick I can barely make out the words.

"Time to kiss me good morning." I peck her on the tip of the nose.

"We should really discuss the jet lag protocol," she mumbles. "You kept me up all night and my body is accustomed to this time zone. Don't be so cruel just because you're wide awake." A small smile is already breaking on her face.

I push myself up a little to see the alarm clock on her side of the bed. "It's eight thirty, darling. Hardly the middle of the night."

"It's Sunday," she grumbles, then perks up for a split second. "It *is* Sunday, isn't it?"

"It is." I can't help but smile. "Relax."

"That's exactly what I intend to do." She scoots closer to me, puts her head on my chest, and exhales deeply.

"What would you like me to do? What does the jet lag protocol dictate?"

"Just lie here with me." Camille lets herself sink into me a little deeper. She really isn't a morning person. I knew from our weekend Skype calls where she would barely be awake at ten, but it's endearing to witness it in the flesh.

I wrap an arm around her and stroke her hair with the other and, as instructed, just lie there. I have nowhere to be. All my desires are fulfilled. There's no need for me to move while she's sleeping on my chest. I'm here. We're together.

Then I hear a meow outside the door. Iris was not happy that we closed it last night.

"Ignore her," Camille says.

Iris starts scratching the door.

"She's very insistent."

"She'll go away." Camille does not appear ready to tend to her cat. "Just be quiet and she'll think we've gone back to sleep."

I try to settle back into the soft sheets, but the thought of Iris sitting right outside the door, waiting to be fed and petted irks me so much, I need to get up. Perhaps it would be different if she wasn't the most affectionate cat I've come across.

"*Mon dieu*, she has adopted you already," Camille said last night after dinner when Iris hopped into my lap as if it were the lap she'd been curling up in for years, and promptly started purring.

I kiss Camille on the crown of her head and try to wriggle myself from underneath her without bothering her, which is impossible because she's lying half on top of me.

"I can't believe you're leaving me for my cat," she says as she rolls onto her back. "You only just got here and she's already got you wrapped around her paw. If you go out and feed her now, she'll know she has successfully manipulated you and she'll do it again and again."

"Go back to sleep. I'll bring you some coffee later." I sit on the edge of the bed, unable to drag myself away from Camille, it seems. I stroke her cheek with the back of my hand and a flood of images of all the things we did yesterday comes rushing back to me.

"The cat food is below the sink," Camille says. She's the one who seems to be purring underneath my touch now.

"Okay." I kiss her cheek, find a robe hanging on the back of the door, and greet Iris outside the bedroom. She nearly makes me trip when she pushes herself against my shins as I make my way down to the kitchen.

CHAPTER TWENTY-ONE

Camille has taken Monday off work and through the magical powers of the French employment system, she'll be able to take three more weeks off while I'm in Paris, even though she has already had two months off earlier this year for her sabbatical journey through Australia. One is reserved for when we go to her family's house in Provence, another for my last week when we'll want to spend every waking minute together, and the remaining five days to sprinkle throughout the weeks I'm here so she'll never be at work for a full week.

We have finally ventured into town and it's a glorious summer day with a blue sky above us and the Eiffel Tower watching over us wherever we go. We're having lunch on the terrace of a café called Les Etoiles in an area called Le Marais, a bottle of heavenly light rosé wine in a bucket next to us.

"The first thing I missed about Australia when I came back to Paris was space," Camille says, pointing at how closely crammed together the terrace tables are. "Everything is so vast and expansive. Except in Sydney. That Airbnb I stayed in was a lot like a typical Paris apartment, really." She smiles at me.

"I wouldn't know. I haven't actually been inside a typical Paris apartment. Spending the weekend at your house might have given me the wrong idea."

"I'll take you to Flo's soon enough. You'll know what I mean." She leans back in her chair, eyes trained on the street.

"While it's true there are a lot of great museums in Paris and a lot of wonderful things to do, this is my very favorite activity and this is my preferred spot to do it from: people watching." She puts a hand on my knee. "I'm elated to be able to do it with you."

I sip from my wine and gaze at the people walking by on the narrow sidewalk. I could easily sit here with Camille for hours, watching, talking, drinking.

"This neighborhood has changed a lot over the decades I've been coming here. It has become much more touristy." She points to the street to our right. "All those big brand name shops over there used to be little, independent stores. But times change. It still makes for interesting people watching though. Parisians are endlessly fascinating to observe, of course, but I love the mix of nationalities you get here. One of my favorite games is to guess which country someone is from."

We play Camille's favorite game for a while, which soon spirals into making up wild stories about the passers-by. When the bottle of wine is finished, we walk to the Seine hand-in-hand, and I'm floored by the incredible beauty of this city once again. Everywhere I look, there's something gorgeous to see. Be it the bridges across the river, the Haussmann buildings along the avenue, or the woman leading me through it all by her hand.

"This city suits you," she says. "You effortlessly look like you belong."

"That's because I'm here with you." We stop in the middle of a bridge and look out over the water. I remember when I came here with Rebecca all those years ago, we were both pleasantly surprised by the sheer number of drop-dead gorgeous women we saw in the span of five minutes, no matter which part of the city we were in.

"Nonsense." Camille stands close to me and kisses me on the lips.

"What was it like to grow up here?"

Camille shrugs. "You take it for granted. And you think every other place on earth is like this. I guess that's why I never left. Once I really appreciated how special Paris is, I didn't want to go anywhere else. Things are different these days, however. A lot of young people are leaving. There are no jobs. I wouldn't be surprised if Ben went to explore the world more after he finishes university. I wouldn't hold it against him either. There's so much to see."

"I've traveled around a bit, but I've never seen a city so stunning. It's just the scale of it that blows you away. It's not just a pretty square here and a splendid cathedral over there, it's everything together. That's so very rare."

"We did some things right in the past. City planning, for instance." She points to a building in the distance with a French flag perched on top. "That's the Assemblée nationale over there. We can only hope its members won't stand too much in Dominique's way of trying to do right by our country."

"Look who gets to talk about the president by casually mentioning her first name."

Camille bumps her shoulder into mine and takes me by the hand again. "Come on. I want to take you somewhere else. I didn't ask you to wear those shoes for nothing."

———

After Camille has guided me away from the river and the big boulevards, she takes me inside a narrow building and down a flight of stairs.

"This is very old school," she says as we descend.

The deeper we go into the building, the louder the music becomes. When she opens the door a French song bellows out to us.

"You can't really know a woman until you've danced with her," she shouts into my ear.

I look across the darkened room. About a dozen couples are on the small dance floor, engaged in what to my untrained eyes looks like a tango. Small round tables line the walls and there's a bar at the back with an improvised DJ booth next to it. All of this would make more sense if it wasn't the middle of the afternoon.

"What is this place?" I look at Camille, unable to hide my bewilderment.

"One of Paris' best kept secrets." She shoots me a wide grin. "It's a *thé dansant*, an old-fashioned tea dance, except we don't drink tea." She grabs me by the hand. "Come on, let's get a drink. Get you used to the vibe of the place. It can be a bit overwhelming." At the bar, she puts a hand in the small of my back, and I feel a little less overwhelmed—I guess she could read it off my face.

"Do you know anyone here?" I ask when we've found a table and she's poured me a glass of wine from the bottle of white she bought.

"I know most of these people." She points at two men who are completely engrossed in their bout of tango together. "That's Pierre and Yves, they run this place." Then she nods at a woman who just twirled past us. "And that's Jeanne, who introduced me to it. I've been coming here for years."

"They seem to take their dancing seriously." I can't get over the expression the dancers' faces are drawn into. All poise and focus.

"That's because dancing is both fun and a serious business." Camille stares at me. "Tell me, Zoya, what's your favorite dance?" She says my name in that way that makes me go all soft on the inside.

"I have some rhythm in me but I've never taken any lessons." Something has changed in Camille's eyes. Something that makes me want to press my body against hers on that dance floor.

"We're good to go then. After the tango, there's usually a salsa. Just trust me and follow my lead."

I burst out into a chuckle. "Do you really expect me to just get up and dance a salsa with you?"

She nods. "That's how you'll learn. The music, the atmosphere… you won't be able to stop once you begin. I'm willing to wager on that right here, right now." She holds out her hand, palm up.

"We'll see." I drink my wine, needing all the liquid courage I can get.

"Just trust me, Zoya." When she looks into my eyes like that, and says my name in such a sultry way, I have no choice but to trust her. I look at her, and at the writhing bodies behind her, and for a minute, believe I have landed in a different dimension.

The music changes and Camille gets up, holds out her hand to me. "Are you ready to dance with me?" she asks.

"Not really," I say, but take her hand anyway.

As we walk the few steps to the dance floor, the two men nod at her, as do most of the other people. No one speaks. This *is* serious business then.

Camille pulls me close, our bellies touching. "Just follow my lead. Start with your right foot back. Listen to the music. No one's judging you."

I try to remember what a salsa looks like again, but I don't have to use my memory, all I have to do is glance around. Next to us, Pierre and Yves are going at it already, looking as if dancing salsa together is all they do in life.

Camille's hips start to move and just feeling her body against mine is enough to bring me into an altered state of being; unfortunately, it's not a state in which I've magically become a master of salsa. I step on her toes and she steps on mine when my feet don't move quickly enough, but while I grimace and burst out into giggles of embarrassment, Camille's facial expression remains solemn and calm. She's teaching me.

It's difficult to feel the actual thrill of dancing with her when I keep tripping over my feet. Even my sense of rhythm seems to have deserted me.

Camille leans over and whispers in my ear. "Listen to

the music, *chérie*. Just let go."

I'm compelled to look into her eyes, away from my stumbling feet, and I do what she tells me. I listen to the music. Another song I've never heard before, but it sounds as though it was composed for one purpose only: for Parisians to dance salsa to on a Sunday afternoon.

I'm not a Parisian, but I'm here with one. The most beautiful woman in Paris, there's no doubt in my mind. A woman who is trying to guide my feet in the desired direction by sheer willpower. It's not exactly working just yet, but I am starting to get the hang of the pattern my feet are meant to make. Right back. Left front. A little hop in-between. I stop glancing around me at the advanced grinding everyone else is involved in. I listen to the music and focus on my steps while looking into Camille's eyes. The subtle shift of her hips on every change of feet gets through to me better and I start following her lead. She presses her belly closer against mine, so the beat of the music moves through us simultaneously, and a smile appears on her face.

When she smiles at me like that, as if I'm the only person in the room—in the world even—it's not that difficult for me to let go and just let her hips and the music guide me. To switch off my analytical brain and let instinct take over. Because this is as close to a mating dance as humans can come. Once I truly get into the groove of the dance with her, it's the hottest, most excruciating foreplay I've ever experienced.

The other couples are twirling each other around, doing complicated things with their arms, but Camille and I just go back and forth, back and forth. The rhythm is hypnotic and soon it feels as though there is no one here but us. That's probably why hardly anyone looked up when we arrived. They were too absorbed by dancing with each other—an all-consuming activity.

The next song is also a salsa, for which I'm glad because the afternoon wine and my jet lag are starting to catch up with me and I'm not sure I can learn another step so quickly. Or maybe I'm just terribly out of shape and a few minutes of moving on the dance floor with Camille have left me winded.

"You're doing great," she says, curling an arm tighter around me, pressing her breasts into mine. I feel her fingers on my neck in a tight grip, and I consider that I don't mind being led by Camille like this at all. She's showing me her city, her Paris, and the life she enjoys here, making me a part of it.

I've only been here two days, and already I never want to leave again.

CHAPTER TWENTY-TWO

On Tuesday, when Camille has to go to work, for which I had to wake her up with persistent kisses on her grumpily cramped-up cheeks, it's just me and Iris in the house. It's strange to be in Camille's house on my own. It makes me feel out of sorts, like an intruder. Because I've only been here such a short amount of time, and these are my first hours without Camille since our reunion, I'm suddenly faced with all the time I will need to spend without her while I'm here.

I remember last year's hiatus from the show, when I was busy trying to salvage my relationship with Rebecca—to no avail. It's different having time off in a house that's not my own, where my routine is non-existent, and my life revolves around another person entirely.

As I walk through the house, Iris doesn't leave my side. Camille was right. She has already started associating me with the new person in her territory who will give her food whenever she meows insistently enough. Camille has given me strict instructions not to spoil the cat in her absence. "Besides," she said, "you're in Paris. You don't want to spend all day in the house."

I don't. Not only because the house feels too big and cold without Camille's presence to fill it, but also because I want to see all of Paris that I can.

Yet, there's an unexpected sort of lethargy keeping me inside this morning. An inexplicable unease about what lies beyond the garden fence. When I look outside the window, I could be in an affluent suburb anywhere in the world. But I know that as soon as I close the door behind me, turn the corner of the street, cross the square, and head into the Métro, I will unmistakably be in Paris.

When lunch time approaches and my stomach starts rumbling, I make my way outside, and it hits me that I've never walked the streets of Paris on my own. When I was here with Rebecca we went everywhere together. On all the trips we undertook, we set out on our discoveries arm in arm. But this is not just a trip, I remind myself. This is me visiting the woman I fell in love with. Everything about this is the opposite of a city trip with a partner you've been with forever.

I head to the Métro and decide to go to the Hotel de Ville stop. Have a spot of lunch in Le Marais, where I have at least been before, then explore the Centre Pompidou, until Camille knocks off work. "Five on the dot, for you," she assured me before she left this morning.

It's odd to rely on public transport to get around. In Sydney, I'm so used to taking my car—and sitting in traffic. The Paris Métro isn't the cleanest and the cars are old and look a bit worn. Maybe I should have gone for an Uber after all. Or maybe I should rent a car, which Camille advised me against because the inner-city traffic is crazy pretty much every time of day. She told me I was very welcome to take her bicycle. Maybe tomorrow I will.

On the Métro, the diversity of people is perplexing. Young, old. Tourists from every corner of the world. Announcements in Chinese and Japanese. I always believed Sydney was a very worldly city, but this is something else.

Because the underground was so dark and dank, when I emerge from the stairs at Hotel de Ville, the day seems even brighter than before. I look around, at the Rue de Rivoli stretching out to my left and right, and consider that Paris even manages to make its shopping streets look attractive—not an easy feat. But I'm not interested in shopping. I want to find out what it feels like to wander through this city on my own, to gauge whether I could ever feel at home here.

What started as a seed of a thought in the back of my brain, is beginning to make its way forward. It's not a well-formed thought just yet. Just a sense of something making its presence known in my mind, lurking at the edges of my consciousness.

I walk and I take it all in eagerly. The way the French speak, with so much music in their tone of voice. The elegance of the waiter when I have lunch. How you never have to order anything from the counter here, but everything is brought to you. The way French women dress, which makes me think I should go shopping after all.

I order my lunch in French, for the practice, but it comes out all botched, and I end up saying it in English anyway. God, this language. So distinguished, but so damn difficult. Last night, when Camille was searching for an English TV channel to watch the news on, I insisted we watch the news she always watches. I didn't understand any of it, but from the footage shown, I got the context. Camille translated for me as best she could, and afterwards I reminded her of her promise to teach me French while I was here.

"Everything in due time, *chérie*," she said. "I've already taught you how to dance salsa."

Maybe I shouldn't rely on Camille to teach me French, but take an intensive immersion course while I'm here instead. As lovely as all the French around me sounds, I'm not going to learn to speak it just by sitting here. Because learning French is not even a choice for me anymore. I know I want to. Camille speaks English. Why shouldn't I speak French? Millions of people speak multiple languages. I barely understand my grandparents' mother tongue. Because no matter where you go, English will always carry you through, even in Paris. However, it's not the kind of visitor to this city I want to be, it's not the kind of partner to Camille I want to be. But French lessons are for tomorrow. Today, I have more exploring to do.

After lunch, I head to the Centre Pompidou and am immediately discouraged by the line in front of the entrance. Though a few clouds have come in, the weather is still bright and summery—not blistering like Sydney summers can be—and I decide to walk more. My hips are no longer stiff from Sunday's impromptu dance session, and I can walk like a normal person again—something I wasn't capable of yesterday and for which I was mercilessly mocked by Camille.

I walk and walk, soaking in the splendor of this city, to which Sydney pales in comparison. There's not the same sense of history in my adopted home city, of what happened centuries ago. Moreover, Camille doesn't live in Sydney. And there's the thought again, rushing to the forefront of my mind. It's much more than an inkling now. It comes at me in the shape of a well-formed confrontational question: would I move here to be with her?

If it weren't for my job, I probably would. That's as far as I can get in replying to my subconscious mind's manifestation in my conscious brain. I don't have the kind of job that's easily transplantable to the other side of the world. I present a show that has my name in the title. My identity is so intertwined with what I do, with what I've done professionally for the past decade, I have no idea how I would even feel if that side of me were to fall away. What could I possibly do in France? I don't even speak French. And I'm not the housewifely type who could keep Iris company all day long—besides, I'd spoil the animal so much it'd be the death of her.

That's how my mind is working as I walk along these streets where, if things were different, my future could lie.

For some reason, my mind doesn't allow me to make the same thinking exercise in reverse. Perhaps because it's not up to me to think about Camille's life in those terms. Maybe her son will indeed go exploring the world and he'll end up in

Australia—like many have done before him—and his mother will follow. But Ben has only just started university. And I haven't even met him.

It's musings like these that give this trip a bittersweet undertone. Because, yes, having these six weeks with Camille is an amazing gift, courtesy of my un-transplantable job, and every second with her is pure bliss, but for most people who are in the process of falling in love, this is normal. To get to completely immerse yourself in the exuberance of young love without having to consider practicalities and distance and how on earth you'll cope with the absence again and again.

I've reached a row of government buildings and wonder what the president of the republic is doing today. It's a silly thought. One I would never have about the Australian prime minister, whom I interviewed once, and who was perfectly groomed by his team to come off charming and even witty at times, but who still only struck me as the person I hadn't voted for.

I think about what Camille told me about Laroche's partner Stéphanie Mathis, the much younger PR executive who helped mastermind her victory, and how Camille said being first lady when the president is a woman is a more than arduous task. What I wouldn't give to interview her.

Then my phone starts buzzing in my pocket. Camille's picture appears on the screen.

"*Bonjour, chérie,*" she says. "*Qu'est-ce que tu fais?*"

"*Bonjour,*" I reply. It's the only part of that sentence I understood.

"I'm giving you your first French lesson tonight."

"I'm afraid the teacher might be too distracting."

"Don't worry, the teacher knows how to use that to her advantage."

Hearing her say that makes me wish it was five o'clock already.

"How would you feel about having the kids over for

brunch on Saturday? This would mean that Ben stays over the weekend."

"Of course." Instantly, nerves coil in the pit of my stomach.

"Are you sure?" she asks, perhaps picking up on the nerves in my voice.

"I can't wait to meet your children, Camille." I might be nervous, but I'm also very curious.

"They can't wait to meet you." I still wonder how *that* conversation between Camille and her children went. When she came back from Sydney and told them about the woman she'd met on the last stop of her travels. Surely, they must have asked a million questions, even wondered about their mother's sanity. I'm not entirely sure that Camille isn't holding back a few details for my sake and for theirs—not wanting to alarm me and not wanting to paint her kids in a negative light. I guess I'll soon find out.

"It's a date then."

"I might swing by Flo's after work. I haven't seen Emma all weekend. Would you like to come?"

"Er, yes. Of course." I can hardly say no. And maybe it's a good idea to meet both kids separately. That would give them less chance to gang up on their mother's unexpected lesbian lover.

"If you could make your way to the Porte des Ternes around five thirty, I'll pick you up there."

We chat some more, Camille telling me about how slow the hours are progressing at work today and me talking about my walk, then ring off.

I look at my watch. I'll be meeting her daughter in a few short hours. It used to be that meeting the parents was the biggest deal after encountering a new partner, but with Camille's parents no longer alive, it's her offspring. I start walking a little faster to burn off the nerves.

CHAPTER TWENTY-THREE

Flo is holding her month-old baby tightly clutched to her chest when she lets us into her apartment. Just before we rang the bell, Camille, looking a spot nervous herself, said she had a key but thought it better not to use it today.

As soon as she sees Emma, all the tension seems to drain from Camille's body and she gets that soft grand-parental expression on her face that's all about the new baby in her life.

"*Viens ici mon petit boutchou.*" She holds her hands out to the baby and Flo dutifully hands her over. Only then does Camille introduce us—as though it's a mere afterthought that I'm here as well.

"Pleasure to meet you," I say, wishing I could do it in French. Before Camille picked me up I looked up the phrase in the French course I carry with me everywhere on my phone, and while it's one of the first things to be taught, and I practiced the word *enchantée* countless times, I can't bring myself to say it out loud in this situation. Because of lack of confidence and standing face-to-face with this dark-haired, younger version of Camille, and the reality check of her actually having a family. And the fact that Camille will never leave Paris if it means leaving behind that little girl she's holding in her arms right now.

"And you." Flo says in accent-free English. "I've heard a lot about you."

"And this is Emma." Camille holds her up a tiny bit, but

clearly has no intention of handing over the baby to anyone else anytime soon.

"*Bonjour*, Emma." I've said bonjour so many times since arriving here, it has already become part of my everyday vocabulary. I take the opportunity to stand a little closer to Camille and the little girl who is obviously the apple of her eye.

"How was your day?" Flo asks politely.

I tell her while I study her face for signs of rejection of me being here with her mother, in her home. I don't immediately find any and can't help but catalog that as suspicious. Not even with the best intentions in the world, and the best relationship with her mother, can she accept me so easily. What I do see on her face, however, is fatigue, and sheer relief that we're here. I'm staring at a brand-new mother first, the daughter of a newly out-of-the-closet lesbian second.

Camille and Flo converse in French for a few minutes and while I don't understand the words, it's no mystery they're talking about the baby.

"How about we take this precious little thing out for a few hours so Flo can have a rest and a peaceful dinner with Mathieu when he comes home from work?" Camille asks me.

"Sure."

Now all I see on Flo's face is extreme gratitude. If minding her child occasionally can win me a spot in Camille's daughter's heart, I'm all for it. Even though I don't know the first thing about caring for infants. I'm certain the doting grandmother has got those aspects covered.

"You don't mind, do you?" Camille asks when we're crammed into the elevator with Emma, her buggy, and a bag filled with everything she could possibly need in the next few hours.

"Of course not."

"So?" She tilts her head.

"So… what?"

"What did you think of Flo? She was very friendly to you, wasn't she?"

"For the few minutes we spent together, she was very courteous." The elevator comes to an abrupt halt and we stumble out, Camille holding the baby and me taking care of all the other stuff. My trip to Paris suddenly feels a lot less glamorous.

"Why don't we take her home?" Camille says more than asks. "Then you and she can get to know each other."

Five minutes later, we're in the car. I haven't really found my bearings in Paris yet, but it turns out to be only a ten-minute drive to Camille's house. That's how at six o'clock I find myself in Camille's lounge with a baby in my lap, instead of the much more sensual position I'd been imagining myself in all day while she was at work.

But Emma is endearing like most babies of that age. No longer a featureless tiny mass of flesh, but a veritable tiny person, a girl in waiting, with huge blue eyes and a tug of the lips that could pass for a smile if you were inclined to see it that way. She coos with pleasure every time I so much as lift her from my lap, and her small, clammy hands grab at everything they come across with a surprising fierceness. Her simple, unspoiled *joie de vivre* is infectious and before I know it, I've fallen in love with her as well.

Of course, Iris is jealous of the intruder in her territory so Camille gives her a treat, after which she just keeps asking for more, then walks off in a huff.

"It has been one of the most profound experiences of my life," Camille says after warming up Emma's bottle and sitting down next to me. She gives me the bottle, as if feeding babies should be in my repertoire of things I know how to do automatically just because I'm a woman. "Having that little bundle of joy come into my life."

Camille rearranges Emma in my arms and I bring the bottle to her lips. She starts sucking immediately.

"Having had children of my own and having gone

through all that entails, I never thought becoming Emma's *grand-mère* would affect me so much. I never thought I'd feel such a big rush of love and such a sense of responsibility ever again. And because I've done it all before, now that I'm older and hopefully a little wiser as well, I want to do it better. I want to have more patience with her and want her to know how loved she is at all times. I want to do right by her."

"You want to undo the mistakes you think you made with your own children. It's very common. I've seen it happen with my parents when they became grandparents. Everything my brother and I weren't allowed to have, these kids will have tenfold. I'm not just talking about material things, but affection and time and just the sheer amount of attention they give them."

"It's the circle of life," Camille says wistfully.

"Except when we were little, our grandparents never fussed over us in the way that's fashionable now."

"Our grandparents didn't have time for that." Camille looks at Emma in my arms with a look of such undeniable, unquestionably permanent love, a pang of jealousy shoots through me again. One that makes me wonder whether she'll ever come to Australia again. "Times are different now."

"You're hardly close to retirement." I remind her. "And your foreign lover is in town."

Camille puts a hand on my knee. "And she's currently giving my granddaughter her bottle. If I was the more sentimental type, this would be cause for a tear of joy or two."

This makes me laugh, and makes some of the tension drain from my shoulders. "And this weekend we'll have an adolescent in the house." Another event I'm not sure I look forward to entirely. There are so many people to meet in Camille's life. So many good first impressions to make.

"Ben is a sweetheart. He's the spitting image of his father, but he has a heart of gold."

"I'd be lying if I said I wasn't a little nervous."

"I come with a lot of extra baggage. Children. Grandchildren. Political connections." She gives a chuckle.

"Speaking of, I'm not leaving Paris until I've been introduced to the president."

"You mean there's such an easy way to keep you here?" She strokes my knee with her thumb.

"You know what I mean." I check Emma for signs of fullness but notice none just yet. "Besides, I think you might have been downplaying your Dominique Laroche connection all this time. I think you may know her better than you've let on."

"Even a president needs friends. Actually, let me rephrase that: especially a president needs friends." She puckers her lips together, much like little Emma is doing while she's extracting milk from the bottle. "It's not that I see her more now than before she was elected, but when I do see her, everything is much more intense. The contact. The conversation. Because time is so limited, it weeds out the small talk and boils everything down to its very essence, even seeing friends."

"Ha, I knew you were more than an acquaintance." My voice shoots up so high, it startles Emma and her mouth loses its grip for an instant.

Camille waves me off. "You're making too much of this, Zoya."

"But I will get to meet her?"

Camille nods, her face drawn into a mysterious expression. "You will. I promise."

We spend the next few hours fussing over Emma like two women who have lost their minds and can only focus on the tiny person that has been dropped into their midst. When it's time to bring Emma back to her parents, I'm so exhausted, I let Camille go on her own.

CHAPTER TWENTY-FOUR

Ben arrives on Friday evening and even though I've seen countless pictures of him, when I meet him in the flesh he strikes me as even more of a golden boy. A young man so sure of himself, the fact that his mother has brought another woman into the house where he grew up doesn't seem to faze him in the slightest. When he greets me for the first time with a handshake too firm for a nineteen-year-old, a slick, confident smile on his face, and the allure of a teen movie star who just walked the red carpet, I can only think I'm meeting a politician in the making.

He's very affectionate with his mother, seems to adore her, and his effortless way with her, and as a consequence with me, puts me at ease. I'm beginning to think Camille's children are of the rare enlightened ilk that truly takes no offense to their mother suddenly deciding to date a woman. Or perhaps they have too much going on in their own lives to spend much time obsessing over it. Flo with her newborn baby and Ben with the new chapter of his life at university.

I must conclude that Camille has been an excellent mother who has brought up her children in exemplary fashion—how else can the courteousness, confidence and utter lack of animosity in the two young people I've met this week be explained? And perhaps their father is a much more decent bloke than his philandering would suggest.

As the time for brunch approaches I can't help but think how strange it is to be dropped into these people's lives.

These people I could so easily never have known. When Camille takes me to the market around the corner on Saturday morning to buy food, reassuring me that we will find everything we need for the brunch right there, and we drag an old-fashioned shopping trolley behind us that we fill up as we make our way from stall to stall, I stop and think about what I'd be doing if the smoke detector batteries in the rental apartment hadn't died when they did.

I'd be visiting my parents in Perth. I'd finally be putting the house on the market and looking for a new place to live —somewhere to start my life over. I'd have planned a trip somewhere warm to escape the cold Sydney winter.

I'm somewhere warm now, much warmer in every aspect than I could ever have imagined. I observe how Camille interacts with the stall owners, who all seem to know her by name. She introduces me to a select few, but mostly it feels like I've stepped into a postcard of times gone by because even though farmers' markets are all the rage these days, there's an air of authenticity to this place that makes me believe it has always been here exactly like this.

Camille has invited her best friends Sylvie and Sébastien to brunch as well and they too seem elated to finally meet me. I've put myself in charge of drink pouring and the mimosas are very much appreciated by everyone at the table, not that, unlike me, anyone looked in much need of something to help them relax.

"Dad would have a fit if he saw you add orange juice to champagne," Ben says. "He'd call it sacrilege." Ben lifts his glass and holds it up to me.

"But your father is not here and this way we can drink more before Sébastien becomes too lyrical and Mathieu starts going on about the stock market as if it was the true love of his life instead of my daughter," Camille says.

Everybody laughs and I laugh along, grateful that they've chosen English as their primary language for the day, which Sylvie seems to have the most difficulty with. But she tries, and for that alone I could kiss her. The fact that the conversation is being conducted in English for my sake, makes me want to keep it going as fluently as possible, to the point that I soon find myself asking Flo's husband questions about his job as though I'm interviewing him for television.

"Ideally, we'd move to London. We talked about it," he confides in me. "But now with Brexit all the rules have changed. It's actually better to stay in Paris." He heaves a small sigh and sips from his red wine—he's the only man who considered a champagne cocktail too girly. "Besides, I could never actually tear Flo and now Emma away from Camille." He leans over in order to speak more quietly. "Those two months Camille spent in Australia upset Flo to such a degree I was starting to worry."

"Did I hear my name?" Flo elbows Mathieu in the arm. "Are you gossiping about me." She looks at me. "He'd better only be saying good things about me." She appears much more relaxed than when I first met her earlier this week.

"I was just warning Zoya about how you and your mother are joined at the hip. She has a right to know these things." He grins at his wife.

"My dear husband is prone to gross exaggerations. I can get by without my *maman* for a longer period of time just fine." They exchange some more words in French, then both smile at me. "But she is the only babysitter I trust so far," Flo adds in English.

As if Emma knows the topic has—again—shifted to her, she starts crying. I notice how both Flo and Camille immediately jump to attention, the champagne-induced carefree playfulness leaving their faces.

Ben gets up and makes a calming gesture with his hands. "*Je m'en occupe, les filles,*" he says.

"My godson will make a wonderful father one day," Sylvie says.

I watch Ben scoot off to the part of the living room where Emma's bed has been set up for the day and remember what Camille told me on our very first date. That throughout her life her children always came first. That she silently endured years of infidelity from her husband for their sake. How she put her own needs on the back burner in order to give them the best life possible. Maybe Flo and Ben are just immensely grateful to their mother for keeping the peace all these years and all they want for her now is to see her happy, even if it means being in a long-distance relationship with another woman. With the stranger sitting at their table, making nervous conversation, trying to catch the nuance in the language they're speaking for my benefit but which is not their own.

As thrilled as I am to be here in Paris with Camille, to have spent this first glorious week with her, I wonder if it all won't be too complicated in the end. Mathieu might have been joking but I've only seen them together a couple of times and it is impossible to ignore how close Camille and her daughter are, and the way she lit up when Ben arrived home on Friday evening. She is a woman who has sacrificed for her children, who adores them, and will never be apart from them for longer than she has to, even now that they're adults. It's clear as day that she's one of those women who needs to live in close proximity to her family.

———

A while later, after we've polished off most of the champagne and Camille has brewed a strong pot of coffee, the group has moved to the couch. Through my own growing tipsiness I've noticed how Camille has become more elated over the course of the afternoon, also helped by alcohol, no doubt, but perhaps also by the fact that she has us all in the same place. In this vast house where her grandparents used to live and where her children have grown up and are now reunited for a day.

Sylvie and Sébastien, who live around the corner, are just as lovely, switched-on and elegant as I would have expected Camille's best friends to be. This glimpse into her life, albeit a festive and not an everyday one, teaches me so much about her, and makes me fall in love with her even more. This convergence of our two separate lives on opposite parts of the globe strengthens my feelings for her, and the conviction that I've met a truly special lady—one I never want to let go of.

Camille drops down next to me, her thigh touching mine and as she does, I see Ben and Flo exchange a look. What I wouldn't give to be a—French-speaking, of course—fly on the wall when they discuss their mother's new lover in private later. Or perhaps I'm better off not knowing what Camille's children really think of me.

Camille, who must still be feeling the effects of the champagne, pecks me on the cheek. "I'm so happy you're here," she whispers in my ear, making me feel very self-conscious.

Camille on the other hand doesn't shy away from public displays of affection in front of her children and best friends at all, and while she re-engages in conversation, she puts a hand on my knee and leaves it there. Perhaps she's trying to make a statement to these people she loves most, and who love her, that this is who she is now.

We make plans for Sylvie and Sébastien to have us over for dinner next weekend, to have Emma sleep over next Wednesday evening, and to drop by Ben's apartment in Marseille in a few weeks when we're on our way to Camille's house in Provence.

By the time everyone has left, and Ben has gone into town to meet some of his old school friends, I sink into the cushions completely exhausted.

"They loved you. I can tell," Camille says as she lies down with her head in my lap, looking up at me. "It was a truly wonderful afternoon." She smiles up at me and a rush of happiness blooms in my chest, but as is always the case, it's accompanied by a sense of finality as well. As wonderful as today was, we only have four more weekends together until we're relegated to living ten thousand miles away from each other again. And I already know that the time we'll have to spend apart then will be much harder because of these weeks we spent together in Paris.

"It was lovely." I say, looking into her bright eyes, simultaneously relishing this moment and regretting that we're not in the sort of situation in which we can bring our groups of friends together, see how they mesh.

"What's wrong?" she asks.

"Nothing." I try to convince her with my wide, television smile.

"Come on, *chérie*. I know you better by now."

It's true. She does know me. Because I've let her. I've shown myself to her inside and out, because everything is more intense, more sped-up in our relationship. "I can't stop thinking about when I'll have to leave. About what will happen then and what our prospects are."

She purses her lips together. "That's still so far away. Try not to focus on that."

I shake my head. "I can't. The harder I try, the more I think about it. It hangs over everything I do like this gray cloud of doom."

"Do you want to set a date for our next visit? Would that make you feel better?"

"Yes, of course it would, but it's not that simple. Nothing between us is simple."

"It can be."

"Once my show starts, I won't be able to come to Paris until it finishes, unless I negotiate a longer break in the middle of the season."

"I'll come to you. It'll be my turn again."

"You have a job, too. And you have Flo and Emma."

"Flo and Emma will be just fine without me for a few weeks."

"But will you be without them?"

"Of course, because I'll be with you." There's enough

conviction in her tone for a smile to appear on my lips.

"What time frame are we talking about?" I ask.

She thinks for a few minutes, as do I.

"Christmas," she says. "Surely you get some time off for Christmas and New Year? It'll be even better if you don't have to work."

"I can't have you spend Christmas without your family."

"The kids can go to their father's."

I start to get excited about the prospect of having Camille with me for Christmas. "You could meet my family."

"I would love to." She grins softly. "See, it's not that hard." Her grin shifts into the mischievous register again. "We may have to record a few more videos to get me through."

"We'll see about that." I lean down and kiss the grin right off her face.

While we get lost in a lip-lock that grows fiercer by the second, I wonder if Camille has the same doubts and fears as I have, and if she does, why they are so hard to address. Perhaps because actually tackling them in conversation, working through them with words, would drive us toward making decisions we're nowhere near ready to make. Making plans for Christmas is easy, because it feels long-term, even though, in our particular scheme of things, we're only planning the next time we'll see each other.

But we have five more weeks together, and Camille is shifting on my lap, trying to pull me on top of her, and when she does that, when she tugs at my hands with such intention, the fear evaporates as if it never existed in the first place, as though this is our normal, this is the house we live in full-time together, and this is a regular afternoon in the lives of Zoya Das and Camille Rousseau.

CHAPTER TWENTY-FIVE

"Today's the day," Camille whispers in my ear. I've barely woken up, but the light in the room is already bright and the birds outside are singing their morning song.

"The day for what?" My brain isn't fully working yet. We've been at the house in Provence for two days and arriving here seemed to have flipped a switch in Camille's brain. The one that puts her in unmistakable holiday mood, and makes her want to double her wine intake at dinner.

She reaches for her phone on the night stand and shows it to me. It's a text message in French, that says: *Nous sommes arrivés. Dîner ce soir?*

"We have a dinner tonight?" I ask.

Camille looks at me, her face propped onto an upturned palm. "While I'm flattered that regular sex with me would make you forget about things you previously couldn't stop talking about, I am a little worried now."

I push myself up a bit more. "What are you talking about?"

"Have another look. See who the message is from."

I take the phone out of her hand and scan the screen for clues. "It says *Steph M*," I say. Then the penny drops. "Stéphanie Mathis?" Excitement quickly takes over. "Dominique Laroche's partner?"

"That's right." Camille takes the phone back from me. "What should I reply? Shall I say that you don't seem to have use of all your faculties today? That all the sex has gone to your head and left you indisposed to meet up with them?"

"Very funny." I push myself up into a sitting position. I can't believe this is actually going to happen.

I watch Camille type into her phone while a smug smile widens on her lips. "*Voilà*." She puts her phone away and looks at me. "We'll have to go to theirs. It's a security thing."

"We'll have to go shopping. I have nothing to wear."

Camille shakes her head. "You have plenty to wear."

I ignore her and prattle on. "And I need to do some research."

"*Chérie*." Camille reaches for my hand. "This is not work. It's not an interview. Dominique and Steph are on holiday. They are here to relax. Let's try and do the same."

"You're going to have to do something to relax me then."

"I believe I can think of some ways." Camille scoots closer and wraps an arm around my waist.

I sink into her warm embrace and try to erase images of Dominique Laroche from my mind, but it's hard, despite the insistence of Camille's lips and hands. It's not every day you wake up finding out you're going to meet the president of France.

———

The way my stomach is coiled into knots as we drive from Camille's to Dominique Laroche's house in a village about ten miles away, you'd think I was about to go into my first TV interview. You'd think I was someone impressed by fame and fortune, instead of the person who, respectfully, tries to pick apart the facade of the people who populate the news—serious outlets and tabloids alike.

Maybe it's because this is a social call that I feel so out of sorts. Or maybe it's just because Dominique Laroche is in a league all of her own. The combination of the stature that comes with being the leader of her country, the way she rose to the top, and the grace with which she seems to move through the highest levels of politics thwarting all the attacks and criticism leveled at her, is like nothing I've ever come across.

"Remember, *chérie*, we're not here for that foursome we talked about. It's just dinner," Camille jokes as she parks in the driveway.

When I look at her, she sends me a wide smile. "She's just a person. Just a woman like us. No need to curtsy either."

Camille's relentless teasing makes me chuckle. She hasn't crossed the line just yet, and I know it's her way of trying to relax me. I must have looked like a student being driven to her first ever exam, the way I sat clammed up in the passenger seat en route over here.

I spot a discreetly positioned security guard to the left of the house, but that's all. As we approach the front door, it gets thrown open wide and two children stand in the doorway. Lisa and Didier, I immediately think, as if I know them. Then a tall, lanky figure appears behind them and I recognize the woman from the many pictures I've seen of her: Stéphanie Mathis.

She says something in French to the children, but they all keep standing there.

"Stéphanie." Camille opens her arms. "*Ça fait trop longtemps.*" She hugs Steph, then formally shakes the children's hands, which they seem to enjoy greatly.

"This is my partner Zoya." She smiles at me, and while I've been introduced as her partner a few times now, it still incites a little tingle in my tummy every time she does, although I guess this one could also be due to the special circumstances I find myself in at the moment.

"Pleasure to meet you." Steph grabs me gently by the shoulders and kisses me on each cheek. "Please, *entrez*. Dominique is on the phone to god knows whom." She quirks up her eyebrows at me. "She'll join us soon."

Steph escorts us to the terrace overlooking the garden.

"I was in charge of making dinner tonight, so I apologize in advance." She paints a grin on her face that manages at the same time to be apologetic and effortlessly seductive. Her dark hair falls in front of her eyes and she brushes the wayward strand away with a casual flick of the wrist. Steph lifts a bottle of wine from the table. "So I shall ply you with some really good wine first. Red all right?"

Camille and I both nod. Christ, I believed Dominique would be the one with the star quality at this dinner. I'm beginning to see why she risked so much to be with Steph. I know the story, of course. And I remember the notorious video they made on the eve of the election campaign frame by frame. But whereas Dominique shone in that, Steph looked ill at ease and as though she'd rather be anywhere else. Tonight, she's all confidence and swag and sophistication.

The stories she could tell. Her English isn't half bad either. I remember the nagging wish I've had to interview her, and an idea sparks in my head. An idea I will have to shelve until later, because Dominique Laroche arrives, wearing a casual summer dress, no shoes, no makeup.

"Camille, *mon amie*." She throws her arms wide and embraces Camille in a tight hug for long seconds while I just stand there waiting, feeling my stress levels rise again, because we may all just be ordinary people, but I do feel as if I'm in the company of extraordinary greatness tonight.

"And you must be Zoya. *Enchantée*." She draws me into a hug as well and then, for a few instances that seem to pass in slow motion, I find myself in Dominique Laroche's warm embrace. Her skin is on mine, her arms pressed affectionately against my back, her perfume in my nose.

"Pleasure to meet you," I mumble.

"We speak English tonight, I gather?" she asks, after releasing me—because that's how it feels. As though I had nothing to do with the impromptu hug and she was fully in charge of when she set me free from it. "Or has Camille already given you a crash course in French?"

"I'm taking classes, but we've only covered the basics so far, I'm afraid."

"Sylvie's daughter Alice is giving her lessons every afternoon," Camille says.

"Lessons?" I say. "I would describe it more as my daily hour of torture. That girl is so strict with me."

"You must be misbehaving then. She's always so sweet to me," Camille says.

Alice is training to be a teacher and everyone thought it would be a marvelous idea for her to teach me a bit of French every day, seeing as Camille's promise to teach me turned out to be a false one, and it would be good practice for Alice as well. It's not so much Alice's strictness that's the problem as my impatience and frustration with myself at trying to learn this new language which seems so impossible to grasp. Having regular lessons is only making me more aware of the vast task of trying to master it.

"English it is then. I don't mind. I need it for my job and I can do with the practice," Dominique says, as if her job is any old job.

We all sit, more wine is poured, and I have to take a few sips before my brain can process that I'm sitting in the beautiful French countryside, drinking an indeed excellent wine, in the company of the woman I fell in love with, the president of France, and her sexy, mysterious girlfriend.

We recount the story of how we met to great glee from our hosts, and for a split-second I wonder whether it would come across as totally ignorant to ask about Dominique and Steph's first ever meeting, but then I remember Camille's words from earlier: this is not an interview, all questions are valid, and no matter our individual levels of greatness and accomplishment, we are all just people. So I ask them.

Steph stretches out her hand to Dominique, and says, "Even though I'll never forget the day she walked into the meeting room at the office, it feels like it happened in another lifetime."

"My life would have been so much easier if your bosses hadn't brought you in to seduce me into hiring their firm for my PR. They should have known you were trouble. I mean, look at you, *mon amour*. It's written all over you. It still is after all this time," Dominique says.

The passion between them is striking. They both seem totally relaxed. Maybe these are the only two weeks of the year they can be like this.

A young woman comes out of the house, and says, "*Didier et Lisa vont se coucher maintenant, Madame.*"

"Ah." Dominique rises from her chair. "Time for bedtime stories. Please excuse me."

"I'll just give them a quick kiss and get dinner ready." Steph follows her inside and when it's just Camille and me on the terrace, I consider how relaxed the atmosphere is, how completely different than I had expected.

"Is she all you imagined she would be?" Camille asks with a smile on her face, leaning over to kiss me on the cheek.

"They are so normal and… in love."

"Hm." Camille just hums. "Dominique is usually a bit more highly strung, but she's on holiday with her children. This is a good time for her."

"It just makes you wonder about the lives politicians are forced to lead. Constant stress and scrutiny. Always having to be ready for something. Never letting your guard down. It takes a special kind of person."

"Tell me about it." Camille rolls her eyes. "My ex-husband was nowhere near being president and just being his wife was often a chore. The endless dinners and misogynistic chatter of the old boys' club to endure. At least Dominique's election has injected some much-needed feminine perspective and ambiance into French politics."

"To be a woman and then come out as gay in that world."

"Dinner won't be long." Steph re-emerges. "I hope you're not expecting anything too fancy. The kids always need all of our attention the first few days we're here. And my natural cooking ability isn't anything to speak of." She smiles that apologetic smile again that is so damn sexy. The hearts this woman must have broken.

This time I do restrain myself from asking the first question that pops into my brain, because it sounds too much like part of an interview. *This must be so hard for you.* It's a bit of a cowardly question that would surely be vetoed before any actual interview on my show, but it's the first thing that springs to mind when I look at Steph.

She looks as though she would be much more at home in a night club, or just casually strolling through a life she constructed for herself by being the person that she is. Anything but having to live with the constraints of a life as first lady to the first female president of her country. Of course, I only know Stéphanie Mathis from what I read about her in the press, but it seems incongruous with the person sitting across from me.

We chat some more about their vacation plans—just chill and do pretty much nothing—and my and Camille's plans for the rest of my stay, and then Dominique comes back out and dinner—a simple but delicious goat's cheese salad—and more wine are served, and slowly my bewilderment changes into a more relaxed state of being, and I forget Dominique is who she is, and I could just as well be having a lovely dinner with a new pair of friends.

After midnight, the wine is still flowing freely—Camille's intake increasing further—and everyone is a little tipsy, but it doesn't matter because we have nowhere to be the day after and it's summer and the woman I love is sitting next to me and the conversation is getting more and more interesting.

"I know you had your reasons, Camille," Dominique says, "but you should have left him years ago."

"You know why I stayed."

Dominique nods. "I do, but look at my kids. They're still so young, and their life, although very privileged, isn't exactly

HARPER BLISS

a bed of roses, but they'll be fine. In a way, it's good for them now that Philippe and I are divorced. That way they can escape the whole circus of their mother being president and lead a somewhat normal life."

"But you see them so little."

"I know." Dominique goes quiet for a few seconds. "But I want what's best for them. Living with their father is definitely best for them right now."

"Do you have children, Zoya?" Steph asks me.

I shake my head. "I do have two extremely spoiled nephews, whom I don't get to see often enough."

Steph nods as though she considers the case closed. "I have two kids now, I guess. Whether I wanted them or not."

"Hey." Dominique swats her on the knee. "The kids adore you." She turns to us. "It often seems to me that they prefer spending time with her rather than me."

"That's because I'm so much younger than you and I actually do fun stuff with them."

Dominique smiles away the playful jab, then taps Steph on the knee again. "I keep trying to convince her to have a child with me after my term is up. Can you imagine a tiny version of Steph? Honestly, he or she would just be too adorable."

"After your term?" I'm too tipsy to suppress my journalist tendencies. "Are you not planning to stand again?"

"Whether I plan to or not is less the question than whether I can win another term or not," she says drily.

"Come on, babe. Of course, you'll be running again and you will win by a landslide," Steph says.

"You have my vote," Camille says.

"No politics tonight, please. Where were we? Oh yes, a little Stéphanie Mathis." She turns to Steph. "I'm not sure the world can handle two of you."

This line of conversation incites Camille to talk about Emma for a while and I glance at Dominique and Steph who are so at ease around each other, so attuned to each other's mild teasing, so informed about each other's innermost thoughts, that I can only conclude that love—and there is a lot of love here tonight—can conquer the greatest obstacles. It gives me hope for my future with Camille.

CHAPTER TWENTY-SIX

By the time the last week of my stay in Paris comes around, I can actually say some things in French and, when spoken slowly and clearly, understand even more. Camille has the week off, and we spend every single second of the day together.

Flo and I have struck up the beginning of a friendship, perhaps mainly based on the fact that my being in Paris hasn't stopped her mother from babysitting Emma. In the past weeks, it has become a habit to stop by Flo's at least every other day after Camille knocks off work, and we've often taken Emma home for the evening so Flo and Mathieu can have a quiet night together.

Because little Emma has lain on my shoulder so often, and I've looked into her wide baby-blue eyes for long stretches of time, I've grown surprisingly attached to her, and I can understand why being a grandmother is such an appealing proposition. Camille gets to spend all the time she wants with Emma—and every so often some time she doesn't want—after which she gets to safely return the child to her parents.

"It's all the good bits without the bad ones," she said once, after Emma had been particularly fussy one evening, and we were both tired and looking forward to some peace and quiet.

I've even grown fond of Alice, my daily French drill instructor, who is a nice girl at heart, and whose task of teaching an Australian woman who has never spoken any other languages in her forty-seven years is not an easy one.

Ben has divided his time off university between Camille's house, his father's, the Provence house, and his apartment in Marseille.

At Camille's insistence, Sylvie has resumed her old habit of dropping by unannounced for a cup of coffee on weekends.

The only person I haven't met is her ex-husband.

I've gotten a good long look into Camille's life and as the weeks have progressed, my conclusion about her never moving away from it has only grown firmer.

A few nights before my departure, with the pressure of time weighing heavily on me, I finally work up the nerve to ask her.

"Could you ever leave Paris?"

"Of course. I'm coming to Sydney for Christmas," she says, not catching my drift.

"I mean permanently."

Camille stops massaging my feet. We're sitting outside on her patio, enjoying a beautiful August evening. According to Camille the summer has been unusually splendid just because I was in Paris. "Is it time for the talk?" she asks.

"Seeing as my plane leaves in about seventy-two hours, I think it might be."

She purses her lips together and stares into the dusk for long minutes. "I don't know, Zoya. It's not that I haven't thought about it. Of course I have, but I can't answer your question in a satisfactory manner. Maybe when Emma is older. Or when Ben doesn't come home so often anymore. It is still kind of early days for us."

"I don't mean to put you on the spot. I just think we should talk about it a little. Have an exploratory conversation of the possibilities."

"How about you?" The relaxed expression she sported while massaging my feet earlier has disappeared from her face.

"Me?" I send her a smile. "I can barely stand the thought of going back to Sydney."

"That's settled then." She smiles back unconvincingly.

"I miss my friends and I miss work, which is not unusual. I always get an itch to go back to work around mid-August. It has become my natural rhythm. But my life was pretty much in shambles when I met you. My relationship had blown up. I was ready to put my house on the market and move to another part of town. I don't have children. What I do have, however, is a job I love. A position in which a lot of other people rely on me. That's something I could never just walk away from."

"I get that."

"What could I possibly ever do in Paris that could give me equal satisfaction? I barely speak the language. And I *need* to work, need to do something. Preferably something like I've been doing for the past decade."

"There are options. I have connections. We could figure something out."

I knit my eyebrows together. "A weekly prime time spot on national television is not easy to come by. I worked my ass off for that spot. If I were to leave Australia, I would give up everything I worked for. And I'm not saying I'm not willing to sacrifice for love, for you and us, because I am, but it's worth taking a moment to consider what it will do to me. As you might have noticed the past six weeks, I'm not exactly *hausfrau* material."

Camille nods, then says, "If I understand correctly, because I don't want to make assumptions, you would be willing to move to Paris for me, if you could find a fulfilling job?" She tilts her head, hope shimmering in her eyes.

I think about this for a while. Although it is the logical conclusion of everything I've just said—of all the thoughts that have been swirling in the back and then the front of my brain for days, even weeks—it does give me pause. "I guess that is what I'm saying."

"We have international news agencies in Paris. Let me ask around if any jobs are opening up for someone of your caliber. This is a pretty worldly city, after all."

"I did have an idea. Not for a job, but something that could earn me a working trip to Paris, but I may need your help."

"Tell me." I can see her perk up.

"I would love to interview Steph for my show. She is such an interesting woman."

"Steph?" Camille whistles through her teeth. "She's also an intensely private person."

"It's just an idea… but my instincts tell me she would make for excellent television."

"Television in which an Australian audience would be interested?"

"No doubt. The entire world has been transfixed by Dominique's presidency. This woman from a conservative party taking out the socialists and the far right in one fell swoop, right after coming out of the closet. To interview the woman she fell in love with would be the perfect blend of human interest and politics. You've seen my show. I'm hardly the kind of journalist who would interview the Kardashians."

Camille chuckles. "I don't think I would have fallen for you if you were."

"French elitism at its worst."

"All jokes aside, I can't give you any guarantees about Steph. I will ask her, but I can't blackmail her with the benefit it would have for us. That's not something I'm willing to use a friend for."

"I'm not asking you to do that at all. I could ask her myself. We kind of hit it off that night in Provence, don't you think?" I narrow my eyes and grin at her.

"There aren't many lesbians Steph doesn't hit it off with, so don't feel too flattered."

"I love it when you're jealous, babe." With my feet still

in her lap, I can't resist tickling her with my big toe.

Camille swats away my toe matter-of-factly. "It would be great to see you before Christmas." There's a twinkle in her glance. "Let me summarize the tasks you have given me, apart from being a loving long-distance partner. I have to persuade the first lady to bare her soul to you on camera and I have to find you a worthy job. Talk about having a high-maintenance girlfriend. Maybe you don't interview the Kardashians because you're aspiring to be one." She runs a finger lightly over the sole of my foot, tickling me to the extent that I have to withdraw it.

"I never claimed dating me would be easy." I maneuver myself in such a way that within seconds I'm straddling her on the bench, which turns out to be a highly uncomfortable position.

"Now you tell me." She pulls me close by the neck and kisses me hard on the lips. When we break from our kiss, she looks me in the eye and says, "Thank you for your willingness to consider moving here."

CHAPTER TWENTY-SEVEN

My plane to Sydney leaves early in the morning and I don't plan to catch any sleep before I have to leave for the airport. I can sleep on the plane—it will beat weeping after saying goodbye to Camille for the next few months. Last night, after a goodbye dinner with Ben and Flo during which she broke the news that she would be away for Christmas, Camille booked her ticket to visit me in Sydney for the holidays. I'm not sure I would be able to board the plane tomorrow morning without the certainty of that purchased ticket. And there's still the possibility of me coming to Paris to interview Steph in the meantime. I called her up and asked. She's thinking about it. Perhaps I'll have a reply by the time I land.

But tonight, it's all about Camille and me. About the physical connection we will miss for long months. We need to make more memories that will last us long enough to carry us through. I don't even care if she wants to videotape us having sex. She can aim three different cameras at me if she so wishes. It doesn't matter. All I want is to have her in my arms, her lips on mine, her soft skin against me, her warm hands all over me. I want to be so intoxicated with her that it will feel as if she's still with me when I board the plane, when I walk into my empty house and pick up my life again.

"Are you all packed?" she asks, standing naked next to the bed I'm already lying in.

"Yep." After one too many shopping sprees while Camille was at work, I've had to leave a few pieces of clothing behind that no longer fit into my suitcase. "Come here." I reach out for her and she takes my hand. She kisses each of my knuckles slowly, almost reverently.

"It's the last time I'll be crawling into my bed with you for a while. I need to take a moment."

Her sensitivity to this moment touches me. Not once during these six weeks together have I gotten the impression that Camille is any less in love with me than I am with her. Before I arrived here I wondered whether things would be different for her without the gloss of holiday and the Sydney sun shining upon us. But it turns out I shouldn't have worried. She taught me the French term for it: *coup de foudre*. I can almost pronounce it without an Aussie accent.

When Camille finally does slip underneath the covers, I feel myself well up. I've gotten so used to having her close, to hearing her breath when I wake up in the middle of the night, and seeing her smile first thing in the morning.

"No cameras tonight?" I ask as I swallow a lump in my throat.

"No distractions," she says. "Besides, I will have no trouble remembering tonight. No trouble at all." She buries her face in my hair.

I wrap my arms around her more tightly, press myself to her. It's a moment of supreme tenderness, before we let this night run away with us. We breathe in unison and even though there are no words spoken between us, we understand what this moment is about. We don't have to say anything. We do enough talking on Skype. Sometimes deep, exploratory conversations that seem to come out of nowhere but, admittedly, mostly just chatting. Not every conversation can be about intentionally getting to know the other, and just chatting has taught me more about Camille than I ever believed it would.

No more words from now on. Words are for later. Now, we just stare into each other's eyes and know how much this means to us, how much we love each other and, perhaps, catch a glimpse of our dreams for the future. As heart-rending as this moment is, it confirms one thing for me: Camille Rousseau is my future.

"I want you," she says. The only words spoken in this bed of silence and tenderness and a love that dances in our eyes and ignites over and over again underneath our skin. I know she means it in more sense than one. I don't just want her tonight in this bed, this gloriously hard king-sized bed which I have had to get used to, and which gives us enough room to sleep soundly, and enough proximity to come together at any moment of the night. I want her in my life. In my thoughts every second of the day.

To find this sort of companionship, this kinship, with another person is so rare, it doesn't matter that I will need to make sacrifices. Because I know that in the end I will. And how can it even be called a sacrifice if this is what I'm getting in return?

Camille runs a finger over my arm and I follow its motion with my eyes. It skates back up and on its next stint downward glides gently over my chest, leaving my nipples hard and wanting. No matter how hungry I am for her, tonight cannot be a frenzy of taking what we'll have to miss, an accumulation of climaxes to savor later. Tonight is all about etching those memories into our brain, slowly and securely, so we will always have them to fall back on when distance does a number on us and times are tough and the longing exceeds our sanity and threatens to drive us crazy.

I let my finger trace its own map of her body, moving my finger from one freckle to the next, touching her pale skin —a week in the southern sunshine hasn't changed her complexion at all. I cup her breast, feeling its shape in my hand, her rigid nipple pressing into my palm. I brush my thumb over her nipple before leaning down and taking it into my mouth, sucking with an unfamiliar gentleness. I want this night to stand out so much, I'm willing to ignore the acute desire that is starting to make its presence known between my legs.

My desire is almost of no importance tonight. Perhaps because I know that, ultimately, it will get quenched in the most satisfying way, and then it will flare up again, when I'm on the plane, surrounded by strangers, and I won't know what to do with myself, but the memory will warm me nonetheless.

I press her body down into the mattress and start kissing my way from one nipple to the other, determined to cover every last inch of her soft skin with gentle pecks, leaving invisible marks all over. *Zoya was here. Zoya loves you.* Marks she would only be able to see when she's in a particular kind of mood. When our love is getting her down and she needs a dose of me. Because as much as I'm dreading my own anguish at being apart from her, I dread hers more. I love her and I want her to be as happy as possible at all times. Knowing that I'll be her source of happiness and unhappiness at the same time is a crippling emotion.

I kiss her shoulders and neck, the sensitive spot just below her ear, and her cheeks as if it's the first time I've ever planted my lips on them. Then I turn her around and kiss the back of her neck, along her spine, the delicious spot where her back curves into her buttocks. I drink in her skin, the tone of it, feel the texture on my fingertips, imprinting it all on my memory—and oh, the memories I've made on this trip. I lie on top of her, pressing my breasts into her back to envelop her body with mine, fold myself over her as though I want to wrap her up in me, take her with me on this long journey back.

When we face each other again, the stroking of our hands has become more insistent. The look in Camille's eyes is different. There's more desperation in them, but also more lust. Our lips meet, while our hands start groping more than stroking. I feel her hand venture between my legs, which I spread wider, while our lips remain locked. Our tongues keep dancing together. I bring my own hand between her legs as well, find them wide already, find her so wet that when my finger skates along her pussy lips, she moans into my mouth.

We break from our kiss and look each other in the eye. She blinks when she pushes her fingers inside of me. Her long, beautiful, glorious fingers. I do the same to her, convinced we can find some sort of rhythm, and that there's enough lust crackling in the air between us, traveling through our bodies and where they touch, that we can pull this off. That we can effortlessly come by staring each other in the eye and fucking each other like this, sideways on the bed, facing each other—each other's mirror image.

The covers have long been thrown off and from the corner of my eye I catch the minute but determined motion of Camille's arm. I not only feel her fucking me, but I see it as well. Not only from the corner of my eye, but on her face as well. A face that lights up as the seconds tick away—as time flees us. She is warm and wet around my fingers, and her fingers thrust high up inside of me, making me gasp for air every time they do. My clit buzzes. Her hands so close to it, but it remains untouched, swelling, craving her touch.

I don't speak, but I slide my fingers slowly out of her and bring them to her clit, hoping—knowing—that she will catch my drift, that she will do the same.

She thrusts up in me a few more times while I try to focus on her clit, which is not easy with her delicious fingers inside of me. Then she follows my example and slides out of me, finding my throbbing clit with a fingertip, and starts circling.

"Oh god," I murmur, because with all this emotion between us, and all this intention behind the action of our fingers, I don't stand a chance.

I see how Camille's face contorts, and I etch the sight of it in my memory, way up there in the list of most arousing things I've ever witnessed, and then I can't control myself any longer. My finger barely moves around her clit as I come, uttering a guttural groan from my throat, inwardly screaming her name, wanting to stay here with her forever, never wanting this moment of extreme bliss to end.

"Please, Zoya," she says, her voice a pleading whimper.

I don't care that I don't get to enjoy much of the aftermath of my climax. Because in all of this, Camille is my priority. I want her to feel what I just felt, and I want her to look me in the eye when she does. I want her to see how I feel about her, read if off my face, where this all-encompassing love I feel for her is impossible to hide.

It doesn't take long for her to start trembling underneath my touch, before she throws her arms around me with a sigh of desperation and says into my ear, "Don't go. I'm not sure I can live without this anymore."

The rest of the night passes in a haze of fingers touching, claiming, driving down deep. In a mess of tears and words spoken that we would, perhaps, never say in daylight.

I drift off somewhere in the middle of the night and wake up groggily to the jarring sound of my phone alarm. And then the time has come for me to go. To leave this bed, this house, this city and this woman for too long a time.

CHAPTER TWENTY-EIGHT

Charles de Gaulle airport is marred by the same kind of chaos as when I arrived in Paris six weeks ago. I remember the version of myself who stood trembling next to the baggage claim belt, so eager to see Camille that my body started shaking uncontrollably. That version of myself didn't have room in her heart and brain to think about this moment, which was only six short weeks away. This dreaded moment of saying goodbye. But this will not be goodbye, or at least only a temporary one. It's an *until later*. Until I Skype her as soon as I get home, when I'll be so jet-lagged I'll be calling her at all hours, and we can dance the time zone tango effectively for a while, until my body adjusts to Sydney time and I'll have to spend my days with her asleep on the other side of the world.

After I've checked in we try to find a quiet spot to have one last coffee and talk, but half the population of France seems to be flying somewhere today, and the airport is so busy, we're forced to huddle in a corner and have our last kiss while dozens of people scuttle past.

"We'll always have last night," Camille whispers in my ear.

"Find me a job soon. I'll take anything to be with you. I'll make tea at the BBC World News office. It doesn't matter."

"Shall I start shopping around that video we made in Sydney? That should get you work straightaway."

I think I'll miss her sense of humor most of all. Who will tease me and push me off kilter for a split second, then make everything right again with a hint of smile or a quick kiss on the nose?

"It's not really the kind of job I'm looking for. I'm getting on. Something a bit less physical would be better."

"I'll see what I can do." She curls her arms around my neck. "I'll see you at Christmas. Once September comes around, the Halloween decorations will start going up, and after that it's straight into the Christmas trees. They'll be up before we know it."

"If I don't see you before then." I waggle my eyebrows.

"That would be a treat, but let's not get our hopes up for that. It's out of our hands. Let's focus on what we can control."

"I can just about control this kiss I'm about to give you." I lean in and kiss her fully on the lips, tongue slipping in deep. Her lips seem softer than ever before, her embrace more loving, her skin warmer.

"*Je t'aime*, Zoya," she says, her voice soft and shaky.

My French has improved beyond the understanding of those words. "*Je t'aime aussi*," I reply.

A group of loud youngsters passes by and rudely pulls us from the romantic moment we were having.

"I suppose I'd better go through security."

"You should. It could take a while. Although the thought of you missing your flight is very tempting."

I toyed with the idea of delaying my flight back, but when I booked it I already cut if very fine before work starts again, hardly giving my body time to adjust to the time difference. Anyway, a few days extra wouldn't have made this moment any easier.

"I'm going now, my love." Instead of moving away from her, I increase the intensity of my embrace, pull her close to me, inhale her smell deeply one last time.

"It's just time and distance keeping us apart," she

whispers in my ear. "They have nothing on our love for each other."

I can only nod at that point as I try to keep the tears that well up behind my eyes from rolling down my cheeks.

One last kiss, a lingering one, and I force myself away from her and walk to the security line in the back of the departures hall. I don't look back as I walk, afraid I will relapse and run to her in an exaggeratedly romantic fashion, which wouldn't be romantic at all, only a prolongation of this miserable moment of me walking away from the woman I love.

Instantly, a deep sense of loneliness takes hold of me. A sensation I feel all the way into my bones, into the deepest parts of me. Because now that I've fallen in love with Camille, my body knows we're not meant to be apart. Every last cell of me is full of this knowledge and the very act of me queuing to go past security is a violation of my body's most fervent wish. To stay. And in that moment, I know for certain my future is in Paris, with her and her family and her friends. I don't feel the tiniest smidgen of joy at the prospect of returning to Sydney. Because she's not there. In my head, I already prepare the defense I will have to give to my friends and family at home when I tell them about my decision. My reasoning that they will try to punch holes into with words of incredulity and a failure to understand what it's like to feel like this. The compulsion to uproot your life, to leave everything you've ever known behind, for another person.

My defense is not very long, but it's air-tight: I love her. Try to argue with that.

When the queue in front of me has dwindled to only three people, I look back. I see a woman trying very hard to hold it together but failing miserably. Even from this distance I can make out the tears streaming down her face. I give her one last wave, then look away, because I have to. This is not how I want to remember her. When I think of Camille I think of her eyes narrowing in laughter after she's made one of her silly jokes. I think of the sounds she makes when she comes and the look of utter surprise on her face every time she does, still now, after all the glorious time we've spent in bed together. As though she still can't quite believe this is who she is now. I want to think of the warmth in her eyes when she looks at her granddaughter, the way her arms soften in preparation for holding the baby in their embrace.

Once past security, a single tear runs down my cheek, but I don't mind. It's a tear I'm proud of crying because of the woman who inspired it. A woman who has changed my life already, and will do so even more.

CHAPTER TWENTY-NINE

"No, no, no, no, no," Caitlin says. "No, Zoya, I refuse to let you move to Paris. I don't care if you're going to be best buddies with Dominique Laroche. You have to stay here. You're my bestie."

"I'm not your bestie. What are you even talking about?" I chose to tell Caitlin after finishing a bottle of wine together. After the extensive wine-drinking training I've had in France, I seem to deal with it much better than her.

"We're BFFs, you and me."

"You're being melodramatic." I wish Josephine were here. She has the precious gift of being able to cut through Caitlin's bullshit with one well-aimed sentence. "Singing somewhere, I gather," Caitlin said earlier when I asked her about the whereabouts of her partner.

"Pull yourself together. This is an important conversation," I say.

"Well, I suppose I can't really hold it against you, seeing as I lived in the US for so long. Tell me though, has Laroche met Trump? And does that drastically decrease my degrees of separation to that orange blob of lunacy? I'm not very happy about that."

"Strangely, it didn't occur to me to ask when I met her."

Caitlin sighs. "I knew you'd go for good. I knew it when you booked your trip. It's just that Sydney will lose a lot of its appeal for me once you leave."

"What's all this sentimentality about, Caitlin? We're

close, but we're not even lifelong friends like you and Sheryl are. And you fell in love here."

"I guess I just missed you. It's been a cold and rainy winter in Oz so far. And Josephine is always busy with something."

"Is she not paying you enough attention? Is that what this is all about?"

Caitlin shrugs. "I guess I could do with a little more. I love to hear her sing, but I don't want to go to every gig. Especially not when she's playing in a dingy student bar in front of a bunch of sweaty youths. That's not very appealing to me. I told her to be a bit more discerning when accepting bookings, but she didn't want to hear it."

"Well, she's not singing for you, is she?"

"Oh, I know. I'm being an ass. But I'm upset because you're telling me you want to leave town. Hell, you want to leave the country and the continent."

"I love her." My most simple and most impenetrable defense. "I guess you would do the same in my position."

"Of course I would. I have done long-distance, even though Boston-New York is hardly comparable to Sydney-Paris, and I know how taxing it can be. But you'll be leaving a good gig here, Zoya. Your audience will be devastated."

My audience. I'm sure Jack, the producer of the show, will try to persuade me to change my mind when I talk to him about my plans using those two simple words that hold so much meaning.

"I've done the show for ten years. Surely, it's time for a change."

"Tell Jack I'm up for it. Or at least try to persuade them to not have you replaced by some boring silver fox male. You've inspired so many women in this country just by being a female on TV, Zoya. You paved the way for many."

"Let's not get too carried away, shall we?"

"Maybe you don't realize it anymore because you've been doing it for so long, but it's true. You've made a difference. You make a difference every single Saturday when The Zoya Das Show airs."

"You'd better stop before you make me change my mind."

"If I'm able to change your mind with what I'm saying right now, then you probably shouldn't go."

"I guess you're making me feel guilty."

Caitlin nods. "Fully my intention." She leans back in her chair. The effects of the wine seem to have worn off a bit. "Purely objectively speaking, when someone with your job and your stature falls in love with a foreigner, it would make more sense for said foreigner to move here to be with you, not the other way around." She holds up her hands. "I'm guessing that's the way public opinion will lean once this gets out."

"She has children, Caitlin. Children change everything. I've witnessed that with my own eyes."

"I'm just playing devil's advocate."

"I also, honestly, don't think I have another five years of the show in me."

"Australia is running out of interesting people to interview, anyway. Even though you haven't even had me on your show yet."

"That's why I have to go to France to interview fascinating people. And I promise you will be on the last season of my show. I couldn't possibly leave without grilling you in front of the camera."

"I'm going to hold you to that promise." She pauses to scan my face. "But what will you do? You can't just sit around all day waiting for your Mrs to get home from work. Folding laundry and cooking beef bourguignon."

"I'll get a job. Or maybe I'll freelance. I don't know yet, but I'm confident it will work out, because it has to. And because I have acquired some skills over the years. Except for that elusive one: speaking French."

"I have no doubt in my mind that when I come visit

you in a few years, you'll speak it fluently."

"What do you mean *in a few years*?"

"Well, when I come visit you next year, you won't be fluent yet. Let's not get carried away. French is bloody hard."

I laugh, then ask her, "So you don't think I've lost my mind?"

"Of course you have. Falling in love equals losing your mind at least for a little while. But you have to do this. What would your life be if you didn't?"

"Thank you." I mean it from the bottom of my heart.

"You're not leaving just yet, thank goodness. You have to tell Jack and Jason and the network and your family. So many hearts to break before you can make your own whole again and live a loved-up life in Paris."

"My mother has been pestering me about finding a new partner ever since Rebecca and I broke up. She'll be over the moon when I introduce her to my posh French lady-friend over Christmas."

"No arguments from me on that front."

"Unfortunately, I have one last season of The Zoya Das Show to complete before I can join said lady-friend."

"But so much to look forward to."

"Yes, like an impromptu trip to Paris next month to interview Stéphanie Mathis." My heart swells at the mere thought of it.

"Major coup, that. You don't happen to need a humble assistant to carry your bags, do you? Or hold the microphone while you're interviewing her?"

"We have people for that." I look into Caitlin's smiling face.

"I'm going to miss you. You're just one of those people I gravitated toward naturally since returning from the States."

"I was so glad to have you become my friend when you did. So you could help me pick up the pieces of my life."

"And look at us now." Caitlin quirks up her eyebrows. "Both of us madly in love with, perhaps, unlikely partners."

"We should probably drink to that." I eye the empty bottle on the table between us.

"Let me see what I can find in the fridge." Caitlin heads to the kitchen, while I think about the broken person I was when she first came back to Sydney less than a year ago, and how quickly things have turned around for both of us.

CHAPTER THIRTY

I book my one-way ticket to Paris while Camille is on Skype with me. I've had all the conversations I needed to have. Some were easier and some harder than I had expected. Jack was surprisingly easy; perhaps he was getting tired of producing my show after ten years of it. My parents' first reaction was sheer devastation—somehow I hadn't expected that. I guess, whatever their age, parents have a hard time letting their children go.

There's a lot to sort out, such as a permanent visa and a job, but I want to book this ticket now. I want to print it out and hang it next to my desk at work, and a copy next to my bedroom door so it's the first thing I see when I get out of bed in the morning. The ticket to my new life.

"Are you sure, babe?" Camille is teasing me again. "Are you sure that interview with Steph didn't go to your head and you're not overly confident about all of this?"

According to Camille, said interview has gotten a lot of air and press time in France, and I might be able to create some work opportunities off the back of it.

"Are you saying you don't want me to click this button and buy the ticket?" I click away from the airline website and look straight into the camera. "Are you breaking up with me?"

"Zoya, please, click the button now." Her voice is earnest. "Please, do it now."

I pause for a second to get another good look at her

face, before I click away from the Skype window and go back to the booking page. I've gone through all the steps. On 5 July next year, in exactly eight months and ten days, I will be embarking on my new life. When Camille comes over here for Christmas and I drop her off at the airport after her visit, our goodbye will still be bittersweet because of the long months we won't see each other, but it will also be full of hope and dreams for our shared future, which will begin later that year.

I take a deep breath. I'm a thousand percent certain I want to do this, but this simple button click is still momentous. Then I press my finger onto the mouse button. I'm asked to confirm. My ticket is booked. I'm moving to Paris. I'm going to live with Camille.

I click back to the Skype window, painting a worried look on my face.

"I couldn't do it," I say. "It's too much. I'm having second thoughts."

"Zoya, please," Camille says matter-of-factly. "I just heard you utter the biggest sigh of relief. Not to mention that I could still see you. I do sincerely hope your future career prospects don't include acting, because you're not very good at it." She smiles widely at me, and then, out of nowhere—not anywhere I can see on the screen, anyway—she produces a glass of champagne. "*À notre futur.*" She raises the glass.

"It's nine in the morning, sweetheart." Empty-handed, I stare at her drinking champagne.

"That doesn't matter one bit. And from the looks of it I'll have to drink for both of us since you didn't bother to prepare the celebration of this big step in our lives."

"I'm still detoxing from all that wine you made me drink when I was there in October."

"All the more reason to prepare yourself properly for your big move to wine and cheese country."

I shake my head at her. "You are incorrigible."

She puts her glass away and brings her face closer to the

camera. "Thank you so very much for doing this, *chérie*. For doing this for us."

"Thank you for staying in my Airbnb and messing with the smoke detector so you could meet the owner."

"The pleasure's all mine."

The rental apartment was snapped up two days after it went on the market. The house will go on sale soon—finally. Rebecca and I will divide the money, and I will have no more property left in Australia, or anywhere in the world. But the only practical matter on my mind right now is that ticket I just booked. I open my mail app and see the new email that has just come in: *Confirmation and E-Ticket Flight Itinerary from Sydney to Paris*.

"Now we can really start making plans."

"It will be all we do when you're here next month."

"Hm, I do hope we do some other things as well." Camille picks up her champagne glass again.

"Of course, we're going to Perth where I will introduce you to my parents and my brother and his extremely loud family. It will be three weeks of utter bliss."

"Your parents who dislike me already because I'm taking their daughter away from them."

"I'll make sure they've properly warmed up to you by then. Besides, one glance at you and they'll know why I want to move to France so badly. They'll fall in love with you so quickly they won't know what hit them. Just like I did."

"And I with you, my love."

I stare at the email with my ticket for a bit longer while Camille chats and I wait for any sign of doubt to set in, but none shows up, and by the time we end our Skype call, every part of me is utterly convinced I have made the right decision.

EPILOGUE

As I travel back in time, because that's what flying away from Australia feels like, the journey feels so different from the two previous times I undertook it. The first time I was so nervous and unsure about what my future with Camille would bring, and if there would even be one after the trip. The second, quick trip to Paris, back and forth in five days to not jeopardize the flow of my show too much, I was nervous and elated at the same time. Elated to be able to steal some time with Camille and nervous because even though I've been interviewing people from all walks of life for years, traveling to Paris to interview Stéphanie Mathis felt special. Not only because of her partner, or because of her connection to Camille, but mostly because of the impression she made on me when we first met. I was charmed and intrigued and inspired all at the same time.

Today, as I fly into the night, I know I won't be able to sleep, and I'm much too agitated to even consider focusing on my French course. I spend most of the journey staring ahead of me, unable to believe this is actually happening. I'm on a one-way trip to France. No return ticket. It's just me flying in the direction my life took the day I met Camille. And I think about love and how it can completely take over your life. I think about how life can thrust you into a situation with a stranger, compelling you to get to know them better, because it feels, in your bones, like you have no other choice and your soul knows there is a possibility of happiness.

I think of the life I will lead in France, of which a large part is still unknown to me, because I haven't secured a job yet, and I still don't speak French very well. It's possible too that Camille and I might need to get married for the completely unromantic reason of getting me residency. All of these are things to be discussed while we lounge on her patio or after we wake up lazily together on Sunday morning. While we just—very simply—are together. And it's because of this upcoming proximity to each other, and the surge of happiness it evokes in my stomach every time I think about it, that I know everything will work out. I'm confident that the first few weeks after my arrival will be spent in a haze of happiness and sex and prancing around Paris with a smug smile of pure joy on our faces. After that, we'll see. On verra.

And of course it's scary to be making my way to the other side of the world without career prospects, without my family and my circle of friends, and literally putting my destiny in the hands of another person. But what a person she is.

———

When I step into the arrivals hall, Camille's entire family is waiting for me. Little Emma is, very lopsidedly, holding a banner that says "Welcome, Zoya" and Camille is jumping out of her skin with excitement.

I had no idea she'd be bringing her family along and the sight of them all as I approach moves me, because they want to make me feel welcome on this happy but nevertheless daunting day in my life. The day I leave the past behind and step into the future, wide-eyed and ready.

"There you are," Camille says when I've reached their group, and puts her arms around me, and welcomes me with an embrace that is so tender, so loving and warm, I know I won't be able to face her family—my future family—with dry eyes. But it doesn't matter, because this moment of reunion is the culmination of many moments we've already gone through together. And as of now, we can truly be together. I stand in her embrace for a long time, until the children start whining and whistling and generally letting us know that we're being untoward.

"Two middle-aged women kissing in the middle of an airport," Ben jokes. "What has the world come to."

What has the world come to, indeed, I think, when I loosen myself from Camille's hug and look into her tearful face. It has come to this. Her and me together. The beginning of our life together.

Zoya and Camille will be back in a brand new season of French Kissing that will be released in early 2018.

ACKNOWLEDGEMENTS

As I write this, I'm a couple of chapters into Book Six of the *Pink Bean* series, and I can't tell you what a joy it is to come back to these characters and this place again and again. Even though I've previously written *High Rise* and *French Kissing*, this feels like my first proper series. One I can return to indefinitely if I were to feel so inclined.

The reason it took me so long to take the plunge and devise a long-running series (I've currently planned up to Book Nine), was because I was afraid. I love a shiny new thing as much as the next person (or perhaps even more because I am, after all, a writer in constant need of procrastination material.) It may sound a bit strange, but I was afraid I would bore myself, having to return to the same old characters and the same old place. But the opposite has been true. Partly because every book introduces a healthy number of new characters, but also because the recurring cast now has a place in my heart.

I dream of Robin's rock hard abs and I imagine myself singing like Josephine while Caitlin looks at me in admiration. Every time I order a cappuccino, I wish it was Micky serving it to me and if Amber were an actual real-life yoga teacher, I might actually make it to a class more than once every three years. When I enter a particularly cozy coffee shop, I sometimes find myself thinking: hm, this would make a great Pink Bean.

But more than anything, in this rather tumultuous time in my life (I'm currently traveling and have been prone to massive bouts of homesickness, which are even harder when you don't really know where home actually is), writing this series, and this book in particular—of which I wrote half during our last weeks in Hong Kong and half while on the road in New Zealand—has been such an enormous source of comfort. An anchor, if you will, to tether me to something I know: writing these characters. (And super long sentences with commas abound.) ;-)

For me, *Pink Bean* equals joy. I can't tell you when I last had a bad day of writing. Sometimes it feels like these books just write themselves. Because everything that defines them is such an ingrained part of me now. And even though *This Foreign Affair* is not a book with a big message (unlike the previous three), it's still important because of all the passion and big-heartedness I tried to put into it. Because isn't every romance ultimately about one thing?

Speaking of (love, that is). Lots of love to everyone who has made this a better book. The usual suspects were all part of it once again: my endlessly patient wife, Caroline; my skilled and snarky editor, Cheyenne; my ever-optimistic beta reader, Carrie; every fantastic member of my Launch Team; and of course, you, dear reader. You have given me so much and every single word I write is, ultimately, for you.

Thank you.

ABOUT THE AUTHOR

Harper Bliss is the author of the novels *Everything Between Us, Beneath the Surface, In the Distance There Is Light. The Road to You, Seasons of Love*, and *At the Water's Edge*, the *High Rise* series, the *French Kissing* serial and several other lesbian erotica and romance titles. She is the co-founder of Ladylit Publishing, an independent press focusing on lesbian fiction. Harper is currently on a digital nomad adventure around the world with her wife Caroline.

Harper loves hearing from readers and if you'd like to drop her a note you can do so via harperbliss@gmail.com

Website: www.harperbliss.com
Facebook: facebook.com/HarperBliss
Twitter: twitter.com/HarperBliss

CPSIA information can be obtained
at www.ICGtesting.com
Printed in the USA
LVHW03s1532120718
583537LV00001B/39/P